"What's Going on?" Mrs. Phister asked. "And what *is* that disgusting smell?" She held her nose.

"Someone put a stink bomb in my book bag," Ashley said.

"Oh, Ashley. That's just terrible," Mrs. Phister said. "You tell me who did it, and I'll make sure that person has detention for a week. For a month. In fact, I'll call his or her parents in for a conference." She was looking right at Iggy as she spoke.

I held my breath. If my father found out, I'd probably be grounded until I turned twenty-one. And I'd be lucky if my mother ever spoke to me again.

Books by M. M. Ragz

Eyeballs for Breakfast
Eyeballs for Lunch
Sewer Soup
Stiff Competition

Available from MINSTREL Books

Eyeballs for Lunch

M. M. RAGZ

A MINSTREL® BOOK

PUBLISHED BY POCKET BOOKS

New York   London   Toronto   Sydney   Tokyo   Singapore

A MINSTREL PAPERBACK *ORIGINAL*

A Minstrel Book published by
POCKET BOOKS, a division of Simon & Schuster Inc.
1230 Avenue of the Americas, New York, NY 10020

ISBN: 0-671-75882-9

First Minstrel Books printing September 1992

10 9 8 7 6 5 4 3 2 1

A MINSTREL BOOK and colophon are registered trademarks of Simon & Schuster Inc.

Cover art by Catherine Huerta

Printed in the U.S.A.

*Dedicated to
my godmother, Marie Hartman
with love*

Special thanks to: Helen Casinelli
of Stamford High School,
Beverly Erickson
of Hillcrest Middle School,
and Judith Kelman

Eyeballs for Lunch

CHAPTER ONE

Lunch—one of my favorite periods in school.

"Hurry up, Murphy," my best friend, Peter Patterson, said. "Let's get in the front of the line for the cafeteria. I'm buying lunch today."

"Not me," I said. "I can't eat the glop they cook." I reached into my book bag to get the lunch Mom had packed me and—"Oh, no. Peter, I must've forgotten my lunch at home."

He laughed. "So you'll be stuck with cafeteria food. How bad can it be? Maybe they'll serve pizza. Hurry up."

I pulled an extra large fireball candy out of my pocket, unwrapped it, and popped it into my mouth. It was so big I felt like a squirrel with a walnut in my cheek.

A couple of other classes had gotten to the cafeteria before us, and Peter and I ended up close to the end of the line. By the time we got served our "Meat Loaf Special," all the seats at our usual tables were taken.

1

"I see two seats together," Peter said, heading toward a table in the corner. "Hurry up before someone else gets them."

But I knew no one else would rush to beat us. Across from the two empty seats sat Drool, a kid who had to be one of the noisiest and messiest eaters in school. He was a tough kid, but his personal habits were disgusting.

We sat down and Peter started poking at his mashed potatoes. I took the fireball out of my mouth, but it was still too big to throw away, and I wanted to save it for later. As I blew on it to dry it and put it in a napkin next to me, he said, "You know what, Murphy? I don't think these are really potatoes. I think they take all the leftover pieces of chalk from the classrooms, grind them up, add a little water, and pass them off as potatoes."

I took a bite. "Yuck. They're cold. And soggy. How's the meat loaf?"

Peter tasted a piece. "I don't think it's meat. I think it's—"

"I don't want to hear it," I said. "Whatever it is, it's nasty. It's not fit to eat." I looked over the food that had been plopped onto my Styrofoam tray—mashed potatoes, gray meat loaf with gravy that was all shiny and lumpy, pale green peas, a big square of Jell-O for dessert, and a carton of milk.

Across from us, Drool was practically licking his plate. He made loud, smacking noises as he wiped some gravy from the plate with his finger and stuck it in his mouth.

"That's disgusting," I said to him. "How can you eat that stuff?"

Drool looked up, his finger still in his mouth. A little

2

bit of gravy dribbled down his chin. I was sorry I had said anything. The last thing I needed was lunchtime conversation with Drool. I shifted my eyes, thinking I'd say something instead to the kid sitting next to him. But that was Iggy Sands, the class practical joker. Iggy and Drool were good friends, but I guess even Iggy couldn't stand Drool's eating habits, because he had his back toward Drool and was deep in conversation with Ed Witbread, his other best friend.

Drool pulled his finger out with a big *pop* and smiled a little. "I like the food here. It's good." He scooped the wobbly square of Jell-O onto his fork and shoved it whole into his mouth. Pieces of red dribbled onto his chin.

"Oh, for crying out loud," I said. "Wipe your chin, Drool." I tossed my napkin at him, forgetting that I had put my fireball in it. Just at that second Iggy was turning around and watched as the fireball flew out of the napkin and landed in the middle of his mashed potatoes. I looked around, trying to pretend that I hadn't tossed the napkin, but he knew. I was waiting for him to leap across the table and hit me.

Instead, Iggy picked up his blob of Jell-O and threw it at me. But I saw it coming, ducked, and it flew past my head and hit another kid right in the ear.

He looked at the Jell-O sitting on his shoulder, looked at Iggy, and, without a second's thought, loaded a gigantic lump of mashed potatoes onto his spoon and twanged it at him. But Iggy ducked, and the potatoes hit Ed, who picked up a handful of peas and just threw them. They went everywhere.

It all happened so fast that the whole cafeteria was

out of control before the teachers realized what was going on. Food was flying everywhere. Some kids were screaming and running around or hiding under tables as peas, mashed potatoes, meat loaf, and Jell-O whizzed around. Others who had brought lunch from home joined in, and bits of sandwich, raisins, and even someone's cold spaghetti flew by.

When I saw Ed pick up an almost-full tray of food and look around, deciding which way to chuck it, I grabbed Peter's arm and pulled him under the table with me. Then I saw someone else duck under there with us—Ashley Douglas. She moved in so close that she was practically sitting on top of me. She was one girl I just couldn't figure out. She had been new to our school in September, and she had spent the first part of the year treating me like dog vomit. But then, for the last couple of months, she wouldn't leave me alone. She had started acting all mushy and sweet, and some of the guys had started to tease me. I spent a lot of time avoiding her, but she always seemed to turn up in the strangest places—like under this table.

"Hi, Murphy," she said and smiled. "What are you doing?"

"Playing hide-and-seek, Ashley," I said. Peter started to laugh. "What's it look like I'm doing?"

She ignored my sarcasm. She ignored the fact that I was trying to ignore her, just like I had been doing for the last month. Her smile never faded. "While you're here," she said, pulling something out of her pocket, "I thought you might be interested in this."

I looked at what she held up. "A newspaper ad?"

"Not just any ad," she said. "It's from The Sundae

4

School. It's opening up again soon. See what it says? 'Enjoy the best ice-cream sundaes in town. Opening Thursday.' That's tomorrow. And you owe me a date. Remember?''

Peter was chuckling and poking me in the back. "She's right, Murphy," he whispered. "You did say you'd take her."

I could feel my cheeks turning red. I could feel my scalp getting all prickly. It was what my mother called a "panic attack." Suddenly I heard a whistle blowing somewhere in the cafeteria. Teachers were running around, trying to calm kids down, and I could hear Dr. Harder shouting, "Everyone back to class! This instant!"

"Not now, Ashley," I said. "This is no place to discuss it. Come on, we've got to get out of here."

"Okay," she said. "But I'm not letting you forget." She turned off her smile like she had been hit with cold water. "You said we'd go, and if you try to back out, I'm going to tell the whole school."

"So what? Tell everybody in the world I wouldn't take you to The Sundae School. Who cares?"

She smiled again, but it was a cold smile. "I *could* tell everyone that you tried to kiss me. Or that you call me up at home all the time and won't leave me alone."

"No one would believe you, Ashley."

"You can't be sure of that. Enough people might."

I thought about my reputation and how gossip—even if it wasn't true—could hurt it.

"Don't do that, Ashley," I said, standing up and brushing some crumbs off my pants. "We'll go tomorrow. Right after school. Just don't go blabbing your big mouth all over, okay?"

5

I looked around. The cafeteria looked like a garbage dump had exploded. Food covered everything—the floor, the tables, the chairs, and even some of the kids.

Mrs. Phister, our teacher, came over to us. "I just can't believe this," she was saying. "Look at this mess. Well, at least the boys responsible for starting it will be punished."

I started to panic again. Then I saw Iggy and Ed being led away by Dr. Harder. I could hear them saying they didn't do it and trying to blame everybody else. I thought they mentioned my name, but I couldn't be sure. Besides, I knew Dr. Harder would never believe them. They were always in trouble, and I was never in trouble—well, almost never.

As we walked down the hall, Peter said, "You do realize, of course, how that whole food fight started, don't you?"

"Yes, but I really didn't mean it," I said. "I only tossed the napkin to Drool because he looked so disgusting. I didn't mean for my fireball to land in Iggy's lunch."

"Just like you didn't mean to get yourself into a date with Ashley."

"Don't remind me," I said. "The older I get, the more I can't understand why things don't always work out the way I plan them. Will you help me with this Ashley thing?"

"I'll try. Especially since I'm part of it, too."

CHAPTER TWO

Why don't you just get it over with?" Peter asked as we walked home. "How long have you been putting her off?"

"Since November. That's when I won that dumb contest and got all carried away."

"Yeah," he said. "I remember."

And so did I. Mrs. Phister had run a "Cooperation Contest." Every time a kid in class did a good deed, she'd give us a paper ice-cream scoop to put on a paper cone we made. The cones were all tacked up on the bulletin board. Whoever won the contest would win a superscooper triple scoop ice-cream sundae for four at The Sundae School—the best ice-cream shop in town.

Ashley and I had been tied almost the whole way through, and after a while it was like Ashley and I were the only two running a race. I was determined to win.

It all came down to the last day. We had a project due, and Mrs. Phister was going to give a scoop to the team that did the best job. My partner was Steffie Whiffet, and we had worked really hard, so I knew we had a good shot at getting that scoop. Ashley's partner was Iggy.

Ashley was one scoop ahead of me, but when Steffie and I won, that put me in a tie with her. Then Steffie asked if she could give her scoop to someone else, and I figured she meant me since we were partners. But for some crazy reason she gave it to Ashley. Then, as Ashley was about to pin her winning scoop up, she must have gotten a case of the guilts. Anyway, she made a big announcement that she didn't deserve it, and she pinned it right up on top of my scoop, making me—*the winner!*

That's when the trouble started, and that's how I got myself into this whole mess. You'd think I would have left well enough alone. You'd think I would have accepted my win graciously and invited Peter and my two other good friends, Michael and Greg, for ice cream. But not me!

I had felt so good about winning, and so generous, that when Mrs. Phister asked me who I was taking along, my mouth took control without consulting my brain. I named my three friends and then added two more: Steffie Whiffet and Ashley Douglas. That announcement had shocked everyone, I think—including me. But Steffie had been my partner, and Ashley could have kept the winning scoop, and I was feeling so good about the great project and about winning . . .

Peter broke through my thoughts. "How come you didn't use your prize before this?" he asked.

"I don't know. From the day I opened my big mouth

8

and invited Ashley, she started acting like such a pest that I just kept putting it off. Then The Sundae School closed for the winter, and I kind of forgot about it.''

"But Ashley didn't," he added. "Let's just go. Call Greg and Michael and we'll all go tomorrow after school. And you'd better call Steffie, too. You already told Ashley.''

"Do you think there's any chance she'll forget?''

He looked at me as if I had turned into Mr. Potato Head. "Ashley? Are you serious?''

"Well, at least with all of us going, there's no chance anyone can accuse me of having a date with Ashley Douglas.''

When I got home, I called Michael and Greg and explained the whole thing. Michael said he couldn't wait, and Greg was all sniffly, but nothing could keep him from free ice cream. I even called Steffie, who sounded quietly excited about going. The only person I didn't call was Ashley. I kept hoping if I ignored her, she'd go away. Wishful thinking!

At breakfast the next morning the phone rang. Mom answered it, put her hand over the receiver, and said, "It's for you, Murphy. It's Ashley Douglas.''

"Tell her I left," I whispered.

Mom frowned. "I will not. You be polite to Ashley. We've become good friends with the Douglases.''

My two older brothers started to tease me. Tony, who's nineteen, said, "I didn't know you were going steady with Ashley.''

And Ken, who's twenty-two but acts like he's ten,

said, "You'd better watch it, little brother. There are five hundred thousand germs in one kiss, you know."

The two of them started laughing like they had created some terrific comedy act.

I wanted to punch them both, but Mom was glaring at me, still holding the phone. "I'll take it in the family room," I said and clomped out of the kitchen.

I picked up the phone and yelled, "I've got it! Hang up!" When I was sure no one was on the other end, I said, "What do you want, Ashley?"

"Well, and good morning to you, too," she said sweetly. "I just wanted to remind you about our little date after school."

I wanted to throw up. "It's not a date, Ashley. We're just going to The Sundae School to pay off that dumb debt I owe you. And besides, we're not going alone. Peter, Michael, Greg, and Steffie are coming, too."

"Just so you don't make up any more phony excuses."

I wanted to put my fist through the phone. What a lousy way to start the day—talking to Ashley Douglas. "I *never* made excuses. I've been busy. And besides, The Sundae School was closed for the winter. We'll go right after school."

"It'll be so-o-o much fun," she said and started to giggle. "I'll bring bread to feed the ducks."

"Okay," I answered. "And by the way, Ashley. Do me one favor, all right?"

"What's that?"

"Don't go around telling people we have a date. Because we don't. And I don't want anyone getting the wrong idea. Promise?"

She hesitated a moment. "I won't tell a soul. It'll be

10

our secret. See you after school. We can take the bus to The Sundae School and I'll have my mom pick us up."

When I got back to the kitchen, Mom, Tony, and Ken were gone. Dad was clearing the table. As I pulled on my sweatshirt, I said, "Dad, this is absolutely the *best* sweatshirt I've ever had. Thanks for getting it for me." He had been to the Final Four basketball tournament and had brought the shirt home as a present for me.

He looked at me and smiled. "I'm glad you like it. It looks good on you. Don't lose it at school."

"It'll never leave my body," I said. "Gotta go. I'll be home late, but tell Mom I have a ride." I made sure I had my prize coupon and enough money to pay for the two extra people.

As I ran to meet Peter, I tried to think positive. Maybe the afternoon wouldn't really be too bad. Peter, Greg, and Michael were three of my best friends, and we could ignore Ashley and Steffie and have our own party. Besides, most of the other kids probably didn't know The Sundae School was open yet. And who would go there on a Thursday afternoon? Just as long as Ashley kept her promise and didn't go around telling people we had a date. Peter, Greg, and Michael understood, but I knew a lot of other guys at school who would tease me like crazy if they ever found out.

11

CHAPTER THREE

When I got to school, there was good news and bad news. The good news was that no one teased me about Ashley, so I guess she had kept her promise about not telling anyone. The bad news was that Michael and Greg were both absent—Michael with the chicken pox and Greg with the flu.

"What do you think, Peter?" I asked when I found out. "Think I should call off the party?"

"I wouldn't," he said. "You've been trying to get out of taking Ashley for the last five months, so why not get it over with? The fewer people involved, the better. And we can all go again when Michael and Greg feel better—just the four of us."

That's what I liked about having Peter for a best friend. He always managed to say what I was thinking.

After we went through our morning routine—national anthem, pledge to the flag, and attendance—Mrs. Phister had one of her *big* announcements. "This class has been chosen to take part in a special project," she said. "You may have noticed a lot of workmen lately in the classrooms by the gym."

How could we miss them? They'd been making dust and noise for the last few months.

Mrs. Phister continued. "They have been creating two new classrooms, a home economics room and an industrial arts room. Half of you will spend forty-five minutes a day for the next eight weeks taking a course in cooking and the other half in wood shop. The board of education of Westford feels that young men and women should be well rounded."

The whole class started to get excited. Wood shop—what fun! I started to think about all the neat things I could make—a storage case for my video games, a trophy shelf. Maybe I could even make something for Mom if I had time.

I was so lost in my plans that I didn't hear what Mrs. Phister said next. Then she started to read a list of names. She read Ashley Douglas and Steffie Whiffet and a couple of other girls. When she read out Peter's name, he let out a groan.

I leaned over to him. "What's she reading? I think I missed something."

"The names of the kids who have to take cooking."

And then I heard, "Ed Witbread, Murphy Darinzo, Iggy Sands, and Michael Visconti. You ten students will report to the home economics room, the rest of you to the industrial arts class."

I couldn't believe what I was hearing. *Cooking?* I didn't want to take cooking. I raised my hand. Mrs.

Phister liked me, so maybe I could talk my way into wood shop.

"Yes, Murphy?"

My mind was putting together a pretty powerful argument. "Don't you think it would make more sense for the boys to take wood shop and for the girls to take cooking? After all, they're the ones who will have to cook when they get older, and the guys will have to work with tools."

She looked at me and smiled. I smiled back. A couple of the guys were agreeing with me and Iggy Sands said, "He's right. My father wouldn't go near the stove."

Mrs. Phister put up her hands to quiet us down. She took a deep breath and shook her head. Looking right at me she said, "I'm shocked. Really shocked. This is an age of equality, an age when women go to work and men have to learn how to be house husbands. Besides, some of the greatest chefs in the world are men."

I couldn't argue with that. But I still wished I would be making something with hot tools instead of sweating over a hot stove.

"Our first class will be on Monday," Mrs. Phister said. "You'll meet the instructors and have an orientation. In the meantime, think about who you'd like to work with. You'll all have a partner to work with for the rest of the year. It's a cooperative learning project. Each team will work together and earn a grade together."

Oh, well, at least I'd get to work with Peter, I thought.

But when I talked to Peter about it at lunch, he had other ideas. "Be honest with me, Murphy," he said. "How much do you know about cooking?"

"Me? I'm a great cook."

"Oh, yeah? What's the last thing you cooked?"

I thought a minute. Mom did most of the cooking in our house. My dad had gone on a breakfast-making marathon for me a few months ago, but thank heaven that was over. "I make great microwave popcorn," I said. "And microwave pizza. And I even did spaghetti once, with Tony's help."

"That's what I mean," Peter said. "You know as much about cooking as I do—zap something into the microwave and hope it comes out right."

"So? So we'll learn. It'll be fun."

He looked at me and shook his head. "My grades haven't been so great lately. My parents threatened to ground me if I don't come home with good grades."

"What are you trying to tell me?"

"Don't get mad, but I already asked Agnes Greasling to be my partner."

"Agnes Greasling? Greasy Aggie? Why would you do that?"

"Her parents own a restaurant. I'm counting on her for an easy A."

I couldn't believe it. My best friend, deserting me for a girl, just because she knew how to cook.

After school we met Steffie and Ashley where we had arranged to meet—around the corner so that no one would see us all together. The Sundae School is about a half mile from school, and because it was a nice day, we decided to walk instead of take the bus. The sidewalk was narrow, so Peter and I walked ahead and talked about the baseball season and tryouts. Steffie and Ashley walked behind us. I guess they were talking girl

15

stuff because they kept giggling and laughing. I heard them mention cooking, so they were probably planning to work together.

We all had double ice-cream sundaes with fluffy mounds of whipped cream topped with chocolate sprinkles. By the time I got to the bottom of the dish and there was nothing but slush left, I was feeling stuffed and happy. It turned out to be a nice party. When we were finished with our ice cream, Steffie had to go.

"I brought a bag of bread," Ashley said. "Want to feed the ducks?"

The Sundae School was part of a whole area that included an old-fashioned candy shop, a gift shop, and a small farm out back. They had a pond with a waterfall, ducks and geese, two pigs, a goat, and even a cow. The farm was run by an old man who was called Farmer Brown by all the kids. I had been coming here since I was little, and it was still one of my favorite places.

"Want to?" I asked Peter.

"Go ahead," he said. "I'm just going to look around the candy shop for a minute. I'll be right down."

Ashley and I sat on a rock and started to chuck out some bread. Four or five ducks fought over the pieces.

"See that big fat duck?" Ashley asked, throwing a piece of bread in the direction of a duck that was so fat and shiny he looked like an inflated balloon. "He's my favorite. I call him Wobbles because he's so fat he can hardly walk."

I laughed. "He's the one I feed every time I come here. Wobbles—that's a great name."

We watched as Wobbles went after some bread but was beat out by a slimmer duck.

16

"Watch this," I said and held a piece of bread in my hand. As I walked toward the ducks, all the rest of them scattered, all except Wobbles. He just stood still, watching me carefully. I hunched down and held out the bread a few feet from him.

He took a slow step toward me, then another and another. And as I slowly backed up, holding out the bread, he came close to us. He nibbled the bread right out of my hand, then out of Ashley's. When we were out of bread, he wobbled his way back to the pond.

"I really love this place," Ashley said. "Sometimes when I'm feeling sad, I like to come here. It makes me feel good."

I looked at her. "Yeah, me, too," I finally said. And for the first time since I had met Ashley, I felt like we shared something special.

She shivered. "It's getting cold," she said. "Do you want to go inside?"

"In a few minutes," I said. "Let's stay here just a little longer. Peter should be coming out to meet us. Here, put on my sweatshirt. I'm not cold." I took off my sweatshirt and handed it to her.

She smiled. "Thanks, Murphy. This is a really neat sweatshirt. Where did you get it?"

"My father went to the Final Four basketball tournament with some other coaches. He brought it back for me."

It was a little big for her, but I had to admit she looked good in it. I started to wonder what had happened to Peter when I heard someone whistle. Then I heard a whining voice saying, "Oh, Murphy, how sweet." I spun around. There on top of the hill was

17

Iggy Sands with his hands on his hips, rolling his eyes. With him were the two other guys from school that he always hung around with: Drool, the cafeteria slob who was always wrestling everyone down during recess, and Ed Witbread, who I had about as much use for as a toboggan in July. He was known as the Graffiti King of Westford Elementary—he had the fastest Magic Marker in the East.

These guys could make or break your reputation around school, and I had a feeling, as I listened to Drool chant, "Murphy and Ashley sitting on a rock, k-i-s-s-i-n-g," that it didn't matter that his song didn't rhyme. My reputation was about to be ruined.

CHAPTER FOUR

I looked at Ashley. She was looking at the ground. "You *did* tell someone, didn't you?" I asked. The guys kept whistling and making comments.

When she didn't answer me, I said, "This isn't a date, Ashley. You know that and I know that. But you told someone we had a date, didn't you?"

"I didn't mean anything by it," she said. "Gloria asked me what I was doing after school, and I guess I might have mentioned that you were taking me to The Sundae School."

I looked at her in shock. "Gloria? You mean Gloria Witbread, Ed's sister, the biggest mouth at Westford Elementary? I can't believe you did this to me, Ashley."

Suddenly she sounded mad. "Did what to you? I didn't do anything. I can't help it if your friends are all so childish. I have no control over what they do or what they say." She stood up. "My mother's going to be here to pick us up. Do you want a ride or what?"

The guys had come down the hill and were standing behind us, arms crossed, looking like three young gangsters.

I turned to Ashley. "No, thanks. I'll walk."

"Suit yourself," she said and stomped off.

"So when are you getting married, Murph?" Iggy asked, and they all started to laugh. He dug into his pocket, pulled out a plastic bag of chocolate candy, and started to munch.

Ed broke away from the group and picked up a small rock. He chucked it into the pond, scattering a group of ducks. As he picked up a larger rock, he said, "See that duck over there? The big fat one? Let's see how fast he can move."

I was about to say something when Iggy went over to him and knocked the rock out of his hand. "Cut it out," he said.

Ed gave Iggy a strange look. "What's the matter, Iggy? You got a thing for the ducks?"

Iggy glared at him. "Are you kidding me? I just don't want to be wasting my time hanging around here." He popped the last piece of candy in his mouth, crumpled up the plastic bag, and dropped it on the ground. "We've got better things to do."

Ed slapped him on the back. "You're right, Iggy. As usual. Let's get out of here. It's a place for little kids."

"Yeah," Drool echoed. "Little kids and lovers."

I sat back down on the rock. Wobbles came over to me and nudged my knee with his bill, but I was in no mood. "Scat," I said. "Shoo." And I waved my hand in his face. He looked at me for a minute—I guess he

20

was trying to decide if I really meant it—and then he turned and waddled away.

I heard Peter call my name, but I didn't turn around. He came down the hill and sat next to me. "Sorry it took me so long," he said. "But they have this old pinball game up there, and the repeat button must have been stuck. I played about a gazillion games for only a quarter. Want some candy?" He held out a fistful of licorice sticks.

I just shook my head.

"Hey," he said. "What's the matter? You're not mad 'cause it took me so long, are you? And where's Ashley? I thought we were getting a ride home with her."

I stood up. "I guess we're walking," I said. "Come on. I'll tell you all about it on the way home."

School the next day promised to be one of the longest and most disastrous days of my life. Ed Witbread, the graffiti terrorist, had struck again. In strategic places all over the school were big red hearts that had MURPHY LOVES ASHLEY scrawled inside. There was one in red chalk in front of the school on the sidewalk and a couple in red Magic Marker on the mirrors in the boys' room. I wet a paper towel and wiped them off as best as I could. But I knew I'd never keep up with Ed. Besides, it would be hard carrying a soggy paper towel around.

To make matters worse, Peter was absent, too. My three best friends, all home sick. I felt like I was alone in a strange world with aliens after me.

As I walked toward my classroom, a couple of boys I didn't even know made kissing sounds at me in the hall. And I could swear a bunch of girls were giggling

21

and pointing at me. I decided to ignore them. But when I got to my desk, I couldn't ignore the red heart with MURPHY LOVES ASHLEY that looked like it was bleeding all over my desk. I quickly put my book bag over it so no one else would see it, but old eagle-eyed Mrs. Phister never missed a thing.

She walked over to me and lifted my bag. She looked at my desk and then at me. "And what, exactly, is the meaning of this, young man? Who is responsible?"

"I don't know," I said, feeling my ears get hot. "But I'll clean it right up." I went over to the sink that's in our room, wet a paper towel, and grabbed the cleanser. I scrubbed and scrubbed at the ugly red heart, but no matter how much I rubbed, a faint trace of red was stained into the desk.

As I was throwing away the paper towel, an announcement came over the P.A. "Murphy Darinzo, report to the office immediately." It was Dr. Harder, our principal, and she only made a personal announcement when someone was about to face a firing squad.

When I got to the office, the secretary clucked her tongue at me. "Dr. Harder said to send you in as soon as you got here. Looks like big trouble to me. You kids never learn, do you?" And she chuckled as she went back to her computer. Some people just love trouble.

When I opened Dr. Harder's door, she was sitting at her desk, hands folded, looking like she had just chewed on ten pounds of nails. I hesitated, and she pointed to the seat in front of her desk. I could feel something like a lead ball forming in my stomach, and my palms started to sweat. But I tried to keep my cool.

It felt like an hour passed before she finally cleared

her throat, adjusted her glasses, and leaned back. "I need your help, Murphy," she said quietly.

My mind started racing. What kind of help was she talking about? How come she wasn't yelling, threatening me with detention? Telling me she was going to have my parents in? I had never been in real trouble with her before, but I knew how tough she could be.

The silence hung like a heavy fog. But I wasn't about to say anything. I had learned a long time ago that when teachers or parents or even principals are mad, the best thing to do is to shut your mouth and listen.

She leaned forward. "Somehow I don't believe you are responsible for the disgraceful vandalism that has hit our school. And yet, somehow, you are involved. Those red hearts are all over the building. There was even one on the sign for my parking space in front of the school. I want to know who's responsible. I've already talked to Ashley, but she doesn't know."

My brain went into high gear. All I had to do was tell her that Ed, Iggy, and Drool were doing it. The whole school knew about them—they had been nicknamed the Unholy Three by most of their teachers. For sure they would get suspended, for at least a week. And it would get them off my back.

Then my brain downshifted. Yeah, sure, and a week later they'd be back in school and I'd be chopped meat.

Dr. Harder was looking at me, waiting for an answer. I swallowed hard and looked her right in the eyes. "I'd like to help you out," I said. "But I don't know. I really wish I did, because it's embarrassing—to me, I mean."

She didn't say anything for a while. She just looked

at me, trying to read my mind, I think. "You're one of our finest students," she finally said, "and a class leader. If anyone can find out who's responsible, I know you can."

I nodded my head, trying to look very serious. "I'll do what I can, Dr. Harder. I'll ask around, see if anyone knows anything."

"Thank you, Murphy," she said. "I know I can count on you. Feel free to come in and talk to me anytime."

"I'll do that, Dr. Harder," I said as I stood to go. "And if I find out who's responsible, I'll do my best to stop them."

"Don't do anything yourself, Murphy. Just tell me. I know how to handle them."

As I headed back for class, I knew I had to talk to Iggy—alone. He was the leader of that group and probably the most sensible of the three. I sort of considered him a friend, and I had to get him to put an end to this. Ed could Magic-Marker up the whole school if he wanted to, as long as he didn't use my name while he was doing it.

CHAPTER FIVE

I figured I could get Iggy alone at recess, but when we went out to the playground, he and Drool and Ed were hanging together. Every now and then Drool would break away, wrestle some kid to the ground, and hold his hands together up over his head as a sign of victory. He was a bony kid who wore his hair slicked back and a small earring in one ear. He was shorter than most of the boys in our class, but he was strong. I guess he figured he had to remind us at least once a day that he was no weakling. But most of us were used to him, so we usually didn't put up much resistance when he picked on one of us.

As I watched, I suddenly realized he was headed my way. "Want to wrestle, Murphy?" he asked. I didn't answer because he always asked the same question. No matter what I said, the result would be the same.

He wrapped his arms around me and had me down within five seconds, a record, even for him. He looked at me, disappointed. "What's the matter, Murphy? You sick or something?"

I stood up and brushed myself off. "I'm just not in a mood to fool around."

"Yeah," he snickered. "Except with Ashley. Watch it, Murph. Love will make you soft." And he looked around, figured out who his next victim might be, and headed for Raymond Stubbs, who's at least a foot taller than Drool. I guess he needed a real challenge.

Iggy was standing by himself near the school, looking around. It was almost like he was being the lookout for someone, and I had visions of Ed, somewhere nearby, marking up some wall with big red hearts.

I walked over to Iggy.

"Hi, Murph," he said. "How's it going?"

"That's a stupid question," I said. "You, Drool, and Ed are putting all of your energy into ruining me, and you ask me how's it going?"

He gave me a look that seemed to say "I don't know what you're talking about." But he kept quiet.

"I thought we were friends, Iggy," I continued. "I've done you a few favors now and then. Remember that whole science report I let you 'borrow'? And all that math homework?"

Iggy scratched behind his ear. "Yeah, I know," he said. "But when Gloria told us that Ashley told her that you had a date, we didn't believe it. So me and Drool and Ed decided to check it out. And there you were— just like Gloria said—sitting together looking like you were turning to mush. We just about freaked out."

"So Ed whipped out his Magic Marker and smeared my name all over school while you and Drool told everyone that I was in love with Ashley. Dr. Harder had me in her office this morning. She asked me who was writing my name all over the building."

Iggy stopped scratching. "And you told her?"

"No," I said slowly. "Not yet. And I won't if you and Drool and Ed knock it off. And get those other guys to stop making kissing noises at me."

"Can't."

"What do you mean, 'can't'? You guys would be in big trouble if Dr. Harder found out." I knew she probably wouldn't unless someone told, and most of us valued our health too much. And she'd probably never catch Ed in the act—he was like the Phantom of the Magic Marker.

"Listen, Murphy," Iggy said. "The way I see it, you're the only one who can get yourself out of this mess."

"Me? How?"

"You're telling me you didn't have a date. And that you don't like Ashley. It didn't look that way to us yesterday. But if what you say is true, you'll just have to prove it."

I was having some trouble following Iggy's logic, but I figured it wouldn't hurt to go along with him. "Okay. I'll prove it." I hesitated a minute. "How?"

"Do something."

"Like what? Run around the school with a black Magic Marker smearing 'I hate Ashley' under all of Ed's red hearts?"

"That's a stupid idea," he said. "You'd get caught, and it wouldn't prove anything."

"So what do you suggest I do?"

27

He picked at a scab on his knuckle and looked deep in thought. "I don't know, exactly. Do something to Ashley to prove you don't have a big fat crush on her. Maybe some kind of a joke. Like put a laxative in her sandwich or fill her shoes with shaving cream or throw rotten eggs at her or put a whole bunch of tacks on her seat. There are a million possibilities."

I listened as he reeled off one nasty idea after the other. His mind was like an encyclopedia of dirty tricks. I could just imagine the kind of business he'd go into when he grew up: Vandals, Incorporated. People would hire him to throw pies in other people's faces or let the air out of someone's tires.

"So what do you think?" he asked. "Which one?"

"I don't know," I said. "I don't want to do anything that would actually hurt her—physically, I mean."

"You're right. You don't want her to start crying and squealing." He went back to working on the scab on his knuckle, which had started to bleed. A few seconds later he looked up, snapped his fingers, and said, "Stink bomb."

Iggy's thoughts didn't always come out in complete sentences. But I knew if I waited a few minutes, he'd get around to explaining.

"You put a stink bomb in her book bag," he said. "Like during lunch, maybe. We spread the word to all the guys about what's going to happen, that you planted it, and after lunch, when Ashley opens up her book bag, this disgusting smell hits her right in the face." He started to chuckle at the thought.

"You really think that's a good idea?" I asked.

"It's perfect," he said. "That stink will be soaked

28

into her books and whatever else she has in there. She'll be smelling that smell for months. Kind of as a reminder of you."

I thought it was a gross idea, but if I wanted to save my reputation, I had to play along, at least for now. "Great idea," I said, patting Iggy on the back. "This weekend I'll see if I can get hold of a stink bomb, and Monday during lunch I'll pull it off." I also figured that Iggy and the guys might get tired of their little game by Monday, and I could forget all about this whole mess.

Iggy looked around, surveying the playground. Then he leaned close to me. "Why wait?" he whispered. "Come with me."

I followed him into our empty classroom. He pulled his extra-large book bag out from under his desk. I had often wondered why someone who did so little work carried such a large bag. As he unzipped it, I had the answer. His book bag was like a storehouse of jokes and tricks—a box of pepper candy, phony plastic dog-doo and vomit, shaving cream, rubber bands of all sizes, Vaseline, boxes of tacks.

He rummaged around in it for a while and then held up a small, harmless-looking plastic bottle. He handed it to me and said, "No charge. I consider you a friend. All you have to do is stick it in her book bag and snap off the plastic top. Within ten minutes a smell like fifty people passing gas will fill the book bag and everything that's in it. It's guaranteed to last a lifetime."

I looked at the bottle in my hand. "I don't know, Iggy. It seems pretty mean. Even for Ashley."

"Hey, Murphy, I'm just trying to help you out. I got people willing to pay me five bucks for that. So if you

29

don't care about your good name, hand it back." And he reached out for it.

I pulled it back. "No, I'll do it. Just to prove to you what I really think of Ashley." I was thinking that Ashley deserved it. She was the one who made it sound like we had a date when she promised not to tell anyone. Besides, how bad could a stink bomb be? It wouldn't really hurt her. It was worth it to get everyone to stop talking about us.

As we left the room, Iggy looked around and then whispered, "Lunch. I'll spread the word."

I nodded. "I'll plant the bomb."

CHAPTER SIX

I wasn't very hungry at lunch. I sat by myself, trying to decide what to do. I had the stink bomb in my pocket, and I was afraid I'd set it off by mistake. What a mess that would be. But it wouldn't be any worse than the mess my life was now. I kept wishing Peter were in school. He'd tell me if I was doing the right thing.

Just then some ugly kid I had never seen before put his mouth near my ear and made a smacking sound, so I knew what I'd have to do.

I went up to Mrs. Phister, who was on cafeteria duty. "Could I be excused, Mrs. Phister? I don't feel well, and I'd like to go to the boys' room."

She looked so concerned that I felt guilty about lying. "Are you all right? Do you want to go to the nurse? There's been an awful lot of the flu going around."

"No. I just need to get away from the noise for a minute." The cafeteria always looked like the zoo at feeding time, and the teachers on cafeteria duty always looked frazzled, especially since the food fight.

Mrs. Phister put her hands over her ears. "I can understand that, Murphy. Hurry back. And if you're still not feeling well, I'll give you a pass to the nurse."

I walked out of the cafeteria and straight toward my classroom. I passed a couple of teachers, but no one asked me where I was going. That was one of the benefits of being a good student and a member of the student council—teachers trusted me. I just hoped I wouldn't blow it all by the afternoon. But if I had to choose between my reputation with the teachers and my reputation with the kids, the kids always came out on top.

Ashley's pink book bag was under her desk. I knew I had to hurry. I unzipped it just enough to get my hand in, shoved the stink bomb way down to the bottom, and snapped the cap. I heard a small hissing sound, so I quickly zipped up the bag, shoved it back under her desk, and beat it out of there.

As I went back to the cafeteria, I thought about getting a pass to the nurse. Then I wouldn't have to be around when Ashley opened her bag. But that would have been the coward's way out. I knew I'd have to be there when it happened.

After lunch, as we walked back into class, the faint smell of rotten eggs hung in the air. The girls were making faces, trying to figure out where the smell was coming from.

I watched from the doorway as Ashley sat down at her desk. She reached under her seat for her book bag. I heard Iggy suck in his breath, and he and Drool and Ed crowded closer to Ashley. I tried to hang back, but

32

they pushed me ahead of them. A couple of other kids started to gather, kids that I didn't even know from other classrooms. I held my breath as I watched Ashley unzip the bag.

Suddenly she dropped the bag. The smell of something like old gym socks, rotten eggs, and a sewer all rolled together floated into the classroom. "My bag!" she yelled. "Someone put something in my bag!"

The smell was disgusting. I would have left, but the guys had all crowded around, blocking the door. A couple of girls went over to Ashley and said, "Oh, gross. What's that awful smell?" One girl was gagging.

The guys started to laugh. Iggy and Ed were slapping me on the back. I could almost see the fumes rising from the bag.

Ashley wheeled around and stared right at me. *"You,"* she said. "You did this. Didn't you?"

I put the most innocent look on my face that I could. "Me?" I asked, trying to sound insulted. "You're accusing me?" The laughter of the guys behind me was egging me on. "You probably left your gym suit in there too long, Ashley. You should take it home to be washed." Ed was laughing so hard he started to snort. "Or else use underarm deodorant," I continued. I knew I was going too far, but I was on a roll.

Suddenly Mrs. Phister came in. "What's going on?" she asked. "And what *is* that disgusting smell?" She held her nose.

"Someone put a stink bomb in my book bag," Ashley said.

"Oh, Ashley. That's just terrible," Mrs. Phister said. "You tell me who did it, and I'll make sure that person has detention for a week. For a month. In fact, I'll call his or her parents in for a conference." She was looking right at Iggy as she spoke.

I held my breath. If my father found out, I'd probably be grounded until I turned twenty-one. And I'd be lucky if my mother ever spoke to me again. Of course, I'd be a hero to Ken and Tony—they just loved it when I got in trouble—but who cared what they thought?

Ashley stared at me, so hard that I had to drop my eyes. Then I heard her say, "I really don't know, Mrs. Phister. I honestly have no idea who would do this to me."

I looked up and caught Ashley's eye. I started to smile because she was being such a good sport, but the look she gave me almost froze me solid.

Mrs. Phister told someone to open the windows and then started asking if anyone knew who was responsible, but the girls didn't know, and the guys all acted dumb and innocent. "I will get to the bottom of this," Mrs. Phister said. "And the person will not go unpunished." She looked at Ashley. "But in the meantime, why don't you put that in the hall. When you get home, maybe your mother can get the smell out. I hope you didn't have any good clothes in it."

"No, Mrs. Phister. Nothing of mine." Suddenly her face broke into a big grin. She reached into her bag and said, "Just this. I brought it back to return to Murphy."

She was holding my sweatshirt—my Final Four sweatshirt. The best sweatshirt I had ever owned in the whole world. And it smelled like a garbage dump.

CHAPTER SEVEN

As I walked home from school swinging my sweatshirt and trying to get some of the smell out, I thought of one of Ken's favorite sayings: "What goes around, comes around." I never completely understood what it meant until now.

No one was home yet, so I dumped my sweatshirt on the laundry room floor. I knew that Mom would know how to get rid of the smell—at least, I hoped so.

I tried doing some homework, but I couldn't concentrate, so I turned on the TV. Nothing but late-afternoon soaps and a couple of black-and-white reruns. I flipped to a talk show. Some lady dressed all in black was screaming how anger and guilt could infect your whole life. "Repent! Apologize! Make peace with the enemy!" I turned off the TV.

I thought over what had happened. I wondered if Ashley really blamed me. I decided to find out.

When I dialed her number, she answered on the first ring.

"Hi, Ashley," I said as casually as I could.

A cold silence came through the phone. I was about to hang up and forget the whole thing when Ashley broke the silence. "Are you calling to apologize?"

I didn't see any reason to apologize—that would be like admitting I did it—so I said, "I'm just calling to say—"

She never let me finish. "Well, you can just forget it. As far as I'm concerned, Murphy Darinzo, you've declared war. I'll get even—somehow, some way—when you least expect it." And she slammed down the phone.

Oh, well, who needed her anyway? I called Peter, but his mother said he was sleeping. Then I called Michael to tell him about home economics on Monday and to make sure he would be my partner. He told me that his chicken pox was almost better, and the doctor said he'd be back by Monday or Tuesday. But he thought it would be great to be partners in cooking. I didn't tell him about Peter choosing a girl—I didn't want to give him any ideas.

As I was hanging up the phone, Ken walked in. He gave me a funny look. "God, Murphy, did anyone ever tell you that you stink?"

"Look, Ken, cut it out, okay? I had a lousy day, and I'm in no mood for your jokes."

He came over and sniffed at my shoulder. "It's no joke. You really do stink."

I smelled my sleeve. Some of the smell from the sweatshirt must have rubbed off on me, but I had been around the stink bomb smell for so long, I didn't notice it.

Just then Mom and Dad walked in. Mom had a load of groceries that she started to unpack. Dad was putting some cereal away when all of a sudden he started to sniff. Dad has the world's most sensitive nose. I mean, he's like a bloodhound. He can sniff out bad milk, fish in the trash, dirty socks under my bed—anything that smells a little odd. His nose was working double time, and he started to prowl around the kitchen, just sniffing. Ken and I looked at each other, but we didn't say a word.

I expected him and his nose to zero in on me, but instead he headed the opposite way. He disappeared for a minute into the laundry room and came back holding up my sweatshirt. He looked at me. "What did you do, drop it in the sewer on your way home? Or did you take a bath in garbage?"

And then Tony walked in the door. "Hey," he said. "Who threw a stink bomb in here? I haven't smelled one of those since high school."

Everyone turned and looked at me, waiting for me to say something. I thought for a minute about waiting them out, but it was four to one. I didn't stand a chance.

"There was an incident in school," I said vaguely. "Someone set off a stink bomb. I guess my sweatshirt was in the line of fire."

"That's terrible," Mom said. "When I met Mrs. Douglas in the supermarket a little while ago, she said something about some boys setting off a stink bomb in Ashley's book bag. But Ashley didn't seem to know who did it."

Dad frowned. "I can't believe Dr. Harder would

allow such a thing to happen in her school. I think I'll give her a call in the morning."

"Don't do that, Dad," I said quickly. I could feel panic begin to rumble in my chest. The last thing I needed was an investigation. Dr. Harder would surely interrogate Iggy. I knew I could count on me never to squeal on Iggy, but I didn't know if I could count on Iggy to be so honorable.

"Why not?" Dad asked.

"It's already been solved," I said, trying to make my brain work overtime, which wasn't easy in the middle of a panic attack. "Some kids—from another school. They got caught already. And punished. Honest."

His frown started to relax. "Well, why didn't you say so from the beginning?"

Mom, who was holding the sweatshirt at arm's length, said, "I'll have to hang this on the line overnight and then wash it separately. I'm not sure all the smell will come out. I do hope that whoever is responsible is severely punished."

"He was," I mumbled.

It was a boring weekend. Peter and Michael were still sick, and Greg was away visiting relatives.

Sunday afternoon I hopped on my bike and took a ride to The Sundae School. No one I knew was there, just a few little kids with their families near the pond. I sat on the bench eating an ice-cream cone. Wobbles waddled up and put his head on my lap. He was looking for a handout, but the way he rested his head and looked up at me, it made me laugh.

"You think you're a dog, don't you? Someone should tell you that you're a duck."

Wobbles kept his head on my lap, waiting patiently for me to feed him. But when I turned my head to watch a couple of little kids roll down the hill, he snatched the cone out of my hand and wobbled quickly away. Wait until I tell Ashley about this, I thought. But then I remembered what she had done to my sweatshirt and that we were enemies and weren't talking to each other anymore.

I watched as some kids tossed bread to the other ducks, but Wobbles kept getting beat out by the faster, sleeker ducks.

"You've got to be quicker and smarter than those other guys, Wobbles. Otherwise you'll get beat out all the time," I said. As I was leaving, I noticed a kid making sure Wobbles got a good hunk of bread. He didn't have to be fast or smart, he was getting the sympathy vote. I started to wonder if sad eyes would work on Ashley. Somehow I doubted it.

CHAPTER EIGHT

Monday morning at school when Ashley saw me, she stuck her nose up in the air, turned around quickly, and walked in the opposite direction. So she'd never talk to me again. So what. I was wearing my Final Four sweatshirt, and I could still faintly smell the stink bomb if I buried my nose in my sleeve. It was enough of a reminder of how much I hated Ashley.

As I walked into class, Drool smiled and gave me a thumbs-up sign. Ed snorted, slapped me on the back, and said, "Way to go, Murphy. But I never believed all those rumors about you anyway." I almost laughed. He was one of the main reasons for all those rumors.

Iggy was next. He was wearing an ear-to-ear grin and extended his hand. "Put it there, Murphy. I'm proud of you." As I took his hand, a small jolt of electricity shot through my fingers. Iggy started to laugh as he showed me the buzzer he had in his hand. "Gets them every time," he said. But I knew that with Iggy, friendship never stopped him from trying to get a good laugh.

We sat at our desks, and Peter leaned over and asked, "What's going on, Murphy? One day I was absent, and you've managed to make Iggy, Ed, and Drool your big buddies." He looked over at Ashley, who was making a big point to ignore me. "And it seems that Ashley has put you on the top of her hate list."

"It's a long story," I whispered. "But as far as Ashley's concerned, good riddance. She's one pest I can do very well without, thank you."

Peter looked at me, astonished. "Wow. Friday must have been some day."

Mrs. Phister took attendance, and everyone was in class except for Michael, who would be back tomorrow, and Steffie.

At eleven o'clock, Mrs. Phister took us to our new cooking class. "Behave yourselves," she said and left with the lucky kids who were headed for the wood shop.

The home economics room looked and smelled brand-new. It had five mini-kitchens, each with a stove, a microwave, a sink, a table, and two chairs. A shiny white refrigerator the size of a small closet stood against one wall.

Chairs had been set up in the middle of the room, but we were all wandering around, looking at the kitchens, into the refrigerator, under the sinks. In the front of the room was a hand-painted sign that said RECYCLING IS OUR GIFT TO THE WORLD.

"Good morning, class," said a woman who wore a

41

large white apron and a chef's hat. She was also wearing earrings that looked like loops of dried macaroni and a necklace made of some kind of beans. "Everyone take a seat," and she waved a wooden spoon in the air the way a conductor would wave a baton. Peter and I took chairs next to each other, and Ashley sat as far away from me as possible.

"I am Mrs. Barbage, and I will be your cooking teacher for the rest of the year." She was a small woman who had cheeks as round and red as apples with deep dimples in them.

"I am so happy to meet all of you," she continued. "As I call your name, please take the special button I have made for you."

The buttons were big name tags. When I looked at mine, I almost started to laugh. Around the top was printed RECYCLE and looped around the bottom was the word GARBAGE. My name was in the middle, so it looked like the button said RECYCLE MURPHY DARINZO GARBAGE. But we were all stuck with the same name tag, so nobody could make fun of anybody else.

"Don't lose these," Mrs. Barbage said. "They distinguish you as the students of this special class. I leave every day at one o'clock and the room will be locked. But whenever you need to come in after school, just show the custodian your badge, and he'll let you in. I've made special arrangements."

"Why would we want to come back after school?" Peter asked.

Mrs. Barbage smiled. "For extra clean-up time, if you need it. The main power switch will be locked when I leave, so you won't be able to use any of the appliances. But we only have fifty minutes for class every day. And anything that's not cleaned up by the end of the class must be cleaned up after school. Now—the first and most important thing I want you to know about me is that I believe in garbage." She chuckled. "In recycling garbage, I mean." Maybe that explained the strange jewelry.

"And what that means for this class," she continued, "is that nothing—and I mean *nothing*—is to be thrown away. I believe that *everything* can be reused or recycled."

Iggy raised his hand. "How about eggshells. Do we eat them, too?" He sat back and grinned.

Ed started to laugh. He was about to slap Iggy five when Mrs. Barbage said, "No, Iggy, we don't eat them. But they do have another use. Eggshells can be ground up and used to scrub dirty pots. And there will be lots of those."

Iggy groaned. "I'll have dishpan hands before I'm even a teenager. This class is going to be stupid," he muttered. I don't know if Mrs. Barbage heard him, but she kept smiling and acted as if she hadn't.

"A few simple rules, class, and we'll get along fine. So that you learn not to waste, you will eat what you cook. That way you will learn portion control. And you will learn to expand your taste buds. Some of you probably exist on hamburgers and peanut butter. By the end of the year you may even learn to like such things as liver."

"Liver?" Ed sounded outraged. "But what if it makes me throw up?"

Mrs. Barbage slid a wastepaper basket closer to Ed

with her foot and smiled. "Just try to hit the basket. Remember, your mom's not here to clean it up."

Ed slumped down in the chair.

Ashley raised her hand. "Excuse me, Mrs. Barbage, but how are we going to be graded?" That Ashley—always worried about grades. But I sat up a little straighter and paid close attention.

"It's quite simple," Mrs. Barbage began. "You will be graded on a number of things: how well you follow directions, how well you cooperate with your partner, how clean you keep your kitchen, and how well you manage your time."

Without raising his hand, Ed asked, "We won't have any written tests, will we?"

Mrs. Barbage smiled. "Of course we will. What would school be without a few tests now and then? But they won't be difficult if you pay attention and take a few notes."

Ed and Iggy both groaned.

Peter asked, "Do you taste everything we cook? Isn't that a big part of our grade?"

Mrs. Barbage laughed and patted her hips. "Dear me, no. If I tasted everything, I'd weigh four hundred pounds in no time. The taste grade will be strictly up to you. And occasionally you will taste someone else's dish and give it a grade."

I leaned back in my chair and relaxed. I didn't see any reason that Michael and I couldn't pull an A in cooking. "But enough talking for now," Mrs. Barbage said. "You know you will be working with a partner, so why don't you all choose one now and then go into one of the kitchen areas."

44

All the kids seemed to know who they wanted to be partners with. Ed teamed up with Iggy. Peter, shrugging his shoulders at me apologetically, went over to Agnes. Two other girls, Jen and Sue, who were best friends and spent all of their time together anyway, went into the third kitchen.

Mrs. Barbage watched, smiling, as the class teamed up and headed for a kitchen area. Ashley, who had obviously planned to work with Steffie, went into another kitchen, and I went to the last one. I was thankful that it was Michael and not Drool who was the other boy in class. Being partners with Drool would have been torture.

Mrs. Barbage looked at Ashley and me and frowned. "Why are you each working alone?" she asked.

"Because my partner is absent today," Ashley said.

"So is mine," I said. "But he'll be back tomorrow."

Mrs. Barbage looked from Ashley to me. "Then I think it would be much better if you two were partners," she said. "The two who are absent can begin together tomorrow. Or whenever they come back." And she put her hands on Ashley's shoulders and started to guide her toward me.

Ashley stopped dead in her tracks. "No," she said. "I can't work with him. I *won't* work with him." She folded her arms. "We don't get along."

"And I'm not working with her," I said. "I already made plans."

Mrs. Barbage just looked at us. "Oh, for heaven's sake," she said. "I'm not asking you to get married. Now, stop being so silly and get together."

We both started to argue with her, but she absolutely

45

insisted. "You have to learn to work out your differences," she said. "This will be a good experience."

When I looked at her, I realized it would be no use. She had a look that reminded me of my mother when she's made up her mind. Ashley started to say something, then just shut her mouth and stomped into my kitchen. But she made sure that she stood as far away from me as she could with her back to me. What a disaster this was going to be.

"Take a few minutes to get friendly with your kitchen," Mrs. Barbage said. "Everything you need is there. And don't forget—you are responsible for your own kitchen. Try not to make too much of a mess, and share the chores of cleaning up."

Ashley, who had been banging around our kitchen, raised her hand. "There's no dishwasher," she said.

"There are dishwashers," Mrs. Barbage said.

"We don't have one," said Ed, who was in the kitchen next to us.

"Neither do we," said Sue and Jen together.

Mrs. Barbage held up her hands to quiet us down. "Yes, there are dishwashers in this room. Two in each kitchen, to be exact. And each dishwasher has two good hands to wash and scrub." And she waved her hands in the air.

CHAPTER NINE

We spent the first week and a half in Mrs. Barbage's class going over safety rules and the basics of cooking. We learned how to turn on the stove, how to boil water, how to use pot holders, measuring cups, the mixer, the flour sifter. She demonstrated some simple cooking like bacon and pancakes and let us take turns doing different things. She taught us to check that the electric frying pan was hot enough by putting a drop of water in it and watching it sizzle away. But when it was Iggy's turn to try it, she squealed, "No! Use water from the tap. Don't spit on it." And we all laughed.

Two of the safety rules also made us chuckle: *Don't catch a falling knife* and *Don't lick the beaters on an electric mixer when it's still plugged in.* We also watched a video on sanitation—about washing our hands before handling food, why we should wrap food well and keep it refrigerated, and why we shouldn't put open cans in the refrigerator. There was a whole section on mold and bacteria—pictures of fuzzy gray fur growing on bread and fruit and microscopic shots of wormy things in meat. All of the girls kept saying, "Ooooh, disgusting."

By Thursday of the second week we were ready for some real cooking. "I've shown you all I can about cooking fundamentals, and you've all had a turn trying while I supervised you," Mrs. Barbage said. "Now it's time to start cooking in your teams. From here on you're pretty much on your own. I'll help whenever you need me, but I like my students to become independent. Follow directions, measure carefully, learn by any mistakes you might make. That's the only way to become excellent cooks."

She passed out a photocopied recipe to each team— Chicken with Rice. "We'll start out with a fairly simple meal, a two-day project," she said. "Today you will make the rice and marinate the chicken. Tomorrow we'll heat the rice and bake the chicken. Plan to have lunch here tomorrow. Remember—you have to eat everything you cook."

That seemed to make Iggy happy. "That sounds good," he said. "I hope we make a lot."

We headed for our kitchens. Ashley and I still weren't talking. I took the recipe Mrs. Barbage had given us and read it to myself. Then I handed it to Ashley. She read it. Then we both stood there, glaring at each other.

Mrs. Barbage came over. "You two had better get started," she said. "Time management is very important." Then she smiled at us and walked away.

"Get a pot out," Ashley said.

"You get the pot," I said. "I'll get the rice."

"No, you fill a pot with the amount of water the recipe says. You do know how to use a measuring cup, don't you?"

"Oh, that's right," I said. "You have problems boiling water." And I headed for the cupboard.

She pushed me aside. "Get the rice," she said.

We stood for a few more minutes staring at each other. I finally said, "This is stupid" and went over to the pantry. I measured out a half cup, like it said in the recipe, but it sure didn't look like much. Oh well, the less we cooked, the less I'd have to eat.

As I handed Ashley the rice, I heard Ed yelling in the kitchen next to us, "Do something. It's going all over the place."

I went over to see what was going on. The pot on Ed and Iggy's stove looked like a small volcano—cooked rice was spewing out from under the lid, bubbling down the side of the pot and flowing into the stove. Mrs. Barbage was hurrying over, along with a few other kids.

"What on earth did you do?" she asked as she grabbed a pot holder and took the erupting pot off the burner.

Iggy and Ed were looking bewildered. "I don't know," Iggy said. "It just started to explode."

"And exactly how much did you put in?" Mrs. Barbage asked. "The recipe calls for a half cup."

Iggy and Ed looked at each other. "Didn't seem like much," Iggy said. "I figured it must've been a mistake in the recipe, so I put in half a pot. Ed and I like rice."

Mrs. Barbage let out a big sigh. "Rice expands as it cooks. The half cup would more than double."

She looked around at the rest of us. "Follow directions carefully," she said. "You've had your first lesson in what can happen if you don't. But that's how you learn—by making mistakes."

Then she said to Iggy and Ed, "And you two will have to come back after school to do some extra cleaning up. If you don't clean the mess out of the stove, it'll smell next time you use it."

When I got back to my kitchen, Ashley started acting extra snotty. "It's a good thing I didn't go running off to other kitchens like you did. I turned down our rice and covered it when it started to boil. I also dumped the marinade over the chicken."

"Big deal," I said. "When will it be done?"

"In eight minutes," she said.

"Yeah, and only seven minutes of class left and we still have to clean up."

Ashley looked at the clock. "This is all your fault, Murphy Darinzo. I'm going to get an F in rice because I'm stuck with a stupid partner who doesn't know anything about cooking."

"Oh, is that so? I've spent some time in the kitchen, too, you know."

"Yeah, eating," she said.

There was that urge to hit her. But instead I went over to the stove and lifted the lid. The water was almost gone, so I figured the rice was probably cooked.

"Don't do that," Ashley hollered. "It says you shouldn't lift the lid while the rice is cooking."

"Why not? Is it doing something in there we shouldn't see?" I laughed at the idea. "Is it X-rated rice?"

Ashley didn't appreciate my fine sense of humor.

"Anyway," I added, "it looks done." I dumped the rice into a bowl and covered it. It looked pretty good, just a little watery, but I'd worry about that tomorrow. Ashley, meanwhile, was scrubbing out the pot and putting it away.

When she was done, I went over to the sink, pulled up the sprayer, and washed out the sink. "You left the sink a mess, Ashley," I said. "When you clean up next time, do it right, huh? I don't want to get a lousy grade because of you."

I thought about squirting her with the hose, but I decided that would be too childish.

In cooking class the next day Ashley put me in charge of the rice and herself in charge of the chicken. When I took the rice out of the refrigerator, my stomach turned. It looked like a soggy lump floating in a little puddle of water. I tasted some—it was a little like eating pebbles mixed with rubber cement. We were supposed to heat it briefly in the microwave, but I figured ours would need some extra time. I wasn't sure quite how much extra, but I punched in four minutes. That should be plenty.

Mrs. Barbage was scurrying from kitchen to kitchen. When she got to us, she said, "I'm so happy to see you two working together." She handed us a sheet of paper. "Set your table according to this diagram, and we'll all be eating soon." She hurried away

It was bad enough that I had to cook with Ashley, but sit and eat at the same table with her?

We argued about who would set the table and who would serve the food. We finally decided that we would each take care of our own plate. When I started to dish out rice onto my plate, I knew something was wrong. The spoon got stuck, and I had to work hard to get some rice onto my plate where it sat in a massive blob.

I took a piece of the chicken Ashley had broiled, put it over the rice, and sat down. Ashley sat across from me.

"What happened to the rice?" she asked as she got some onto her fork. She put it into her mouth and made a face. "It tastes like *clay!*"

I cut a piece of the chicken and chewed on it a while. "Your chicken tastes like an old sneaker," I said. "It's all tough and burned."

Just then Mrs. Barbage came over to us, carrying her grade book. "Well? How is it?" she asked, pen poised. "You get to grade the taste of your first meal together."

Ashley and I were nearly choking. I swallowed a wad of rice. My mouth was practically glued shut.

Ashley looked like she wanted to throw up. She started to say, "This rice is the . . ." Then she noticed the grade book. She swallowed hard.

We could hardly talk, but I knew Ashley wanted a good grade as much as I did.

"It's great," she finally said, almost in a whisper. "The best."

I just kept nodding.

Mrs. Barbage looked at Ashley, then at me, then at the glop on our plates. "That's good," she finally said.

"Finish it all." And as we choked down another mouthful, she made a mark in her book. "A for both of you."

When we finished eating, my stomach was rumbling. It was either hungry or complaining about what I had just dumped into it, but the taste in my mouth was so bad, I couldn't be sure.

"You wash and I'll dry," I said.

"I washed yesterday," she answered.

"What did you wash yesterday?"

"That rice pot," she said.

"That wasn't washing. That was rinsing. I don't think you even used soap."

"Yes, I did."

"I cleaned the sink," I reminded her.

"So what? I still washed. It's your turn today. Otherwise I'll tell Mrs. Barbage that I had to wash two days in a row."

"You would, too, wouldn't you?" I said and stomped over to the sink. That Ashley. She made me so mad I couldn't think straight. I turned on the water full blast and suddenly felt the cold water. It shot out of the sprayer and hit me right in the face.

CHAPTER TEN

I was standing there like I was paralyzed, water squirting all over me from the sprayer on the sink. Ashley ran over, turned off the faucet, and started to laugh. She was laughing so hard, I thought she would fall over.

Water was dripping from my ears, my nose, my eyelashes. I was so mad, I was spluttering. "I don't think it's funny, Ashley. Not funny at all."

She stopped laughing and put her hands on her hips. "No, it's not," she said. "Your little plan backfired, didn't it, Murphy?"

"What plan?"

She walked over to the sink and fiddled with the sprayer. "You wanted me to do the dishes, which proves that you wrapped this rubber band around the sprayer. You wanted me to get soaked, but you got it, instead."

I couldn't believe what I was hearing. She had rigged the rubber band, and now she was acting like it was my fault. Unreal! She started laughing again, so I grabbed the sprayer, turned the water on full force, and gave her one good blast, right in the face.

Most of the class were circling around us. "Squirt her again," I heard Iggy say, "Hit her again," and I heard Ed's snorting laughter.

Mrs. Barbage came over. Ashley and I were just glaring at each other, like two boxers before the bell. "Will someone please explain what is going on here?" she said.

"Ashley rigged a rubber band on the sprayer and got me soaking wet," I said.

"You mean *you* rigged the rubber band, but your little joke backfired on you, don't you?" Ashley said.

I took a step closer to her and said, "If I had put that rubber band on that sprayer, do you think I'd be so stupid as to turn on the sink?" I asked.

"All I know is that *I* didn't put it there," she said, wiping some water from the tip of her nose. She turned to Mrs. Barbage. "You'd better let us change partners. This just isn't going to work."

"All the more reason for you two to stay together," Mrs. Barbage said quietly. "Conflicts should not go unresolved. You two will just have to learn to work it out. But in the meantime"—she looked at the puddle of water we were standing in—"you'd better clean up this mess. There are some mops in the closet over there."

As Ashley and I mopped and cleaned, I could hear Iggy and Ed chuckling and whispering. They had been in here alone after school last night to clean up their rice mess. And Ashley and I hadn't used the sink during class before I turned it on to wash. Was it possible that they . . . ?

I put the idea out of my mind. Ashley had threatened to get me when I least expected it. So now she was one up on me. Sort of. Because she looked as wet and miserable as I felt.

Peter and I walked home together after school. When I asked him if he wanted to stop for a snack, he said, "I'm stuffed. That was a great lunch we had today. I'm really enjoying that class."

"You are?"

"Sure. Agnes does most of the cooking, and I do most of the eating."

I poked his stomach with my finger. "Watch it, Peter. It's starting to show."

He laughed. "You're just jealous," he said.

"You're right. I am."

The next week of cooking class passed pretty uneventfully. Ashley and I spoke to each other as little as possible. Our food came out okay, but the taste was never spectacular. We had one written test on safety rules. I studied and got an A.

On Friday we were doing steamed vegetables when Mrs. Barbage said, "Class, may I have your attention, please?" She was standing at the garbage pail, holding something long and green between her thumb and finger.

"Someone has peeled zucchini," she said. Then she stopped talking and looked around, holding the peelings high in the air. It was so quiet I could hear our vegetables steaming on the stove.

Then she reached into the garbage can again and came up with part of a wilted carrot. She held that in the other hand, turning slowly for all of us to see.

Finally she said, "You have no idea how serious this is. Do you realize that most Americans throw away about one-sixth of the food they buy? Whoever threw this away evidently thought it was garbage. But this peel and this sad-looking carrot could have been washed and put to good use—stew, soup stock, a compost pile. Because when you multiply this waste by the millions of households we have in America, maybe you can begin to understand why our landfills are becoming a problem. Pretty soon we'll run out of space to dump our garbage."

We all stood there looking at her. No one knew quite what to say. She was being very dramatic on the subject of garbage.

Ashley let out a sigh. "What a lot of fuss over a wilted carrot and some vegetable peel. I'll bet in the old days people didn't worry about their garbage," she muttered under her breath.

Suddenly Mrs. Barbage said, "Ashley, what an excellent idea."

Ashley looked up quickly. She was surprised, I guess, that Mrs. Barbage had heard her. "What idea?" she asked.

"You've given me an excellent idea for a field trip. I am going to take all of you to explore . . ." She looked around the room for a minute, like she had forgotten what she was going to say. Then she cleared her throat and said, "I am going to take you all to an archaeological dig."

"Fantastic!" said Iggy. "Absolutely fantastic." He looked like he wanted to jump up and down and do cartwheels.

Ed looked confused. "What's a arky . . . whatever she said?"

Iggy stood up, turned to him, and said, "Don't you know anything? It's a place where people dig in the ground to find out how people used to live. They dig up arrows and coins and jewels and—" He turned to Mrs. Barbage. "Isn't that right, Mrs. B.?"

"Absolutely," she said. "And this is a special dig, one that's going on right here in Westford. As a matter of fact, my husband is in charge of it."

Iggy was getting more excited by the minute. "Your husband's an archaeologist?" he asked.

Mrs. Barbage smiled, the kind of smile that made it look like she had a secret. "Well, sort of," she said.

"That's what I want to be," Iggy said. "An archaeologist. I want to dig around in the mud and the dirt and find treasure—gold and coins and valuable stuff like that. Has your husband ever found any gold?"

Mrs. Barbage was still wearing that mischievous smile. "You'll just have to wait and see. We'll go next week. I'll arrange it with Dr. Harder. Bring a bag lunch and we'll stop afterward and have a picnic somewhere."

"Let's just eat with the archaeologists," Iggy suggested.

"We'll see," she said.

CHAPTER ELEVEN

The following Tuesday the ten of us from Mrs. Barbage's cooking class came to school looking pretty grubby. Usually a field trip meant we got dressed up, but Mrs. Barbage had told us to wear old clothes because we might be climbing around dirt piles outside. I had on my torn jeans and a pair of sneakers that Mom kept trying to throw away. Every time she tossed them in the garbage can, I hauled them back out. I finally explained to her that Mrs. Barbage was teaching us to recycle and that saving my old sneakers was my contribution to less garbage. She laughed at me, but she let me keep the sneakers.

Ashley looked at my feet as we lined up to get on the yellow bus. She wrinkled up her nose and said, "They're disgusting. Your toes are almost sticking out."

Her clothes were a lot newer than almost everyone else's, and her sneakers were a dazzling white. I hated to admit it, but she looked really nice in designer jeans and a blue denim jacket.

"You're going to get filthy," I said.

"I'm sure that archaeological digs are very neat," she said. "And I wouldn't be caught dead looking as nasty as you do." She turned her back to me and boarded the bus. She might have looked nice, but her personality hadn't improved any.

It was a warm, sunny day—a perfect day to be anywhere but school. We had all brought our lunches and a cold drink for the picnic. What a great day it promised to be.

Peter and I sat on the bus together, Michael sat across from us, and we joined the rest of the class in singing "A hundred bottles of pop on the wall."

We were down to forty-nine bottles when the bus stopped at a large wire gate. As a man came forward to open it, I read the sign: WESTFORD LANDFILL.

The bus pulled through the gates and drove slowly down a dirt road. No one was saying anything. We were all looking at the mountains of dirt and valleys of garbage on both sides of us with sea gulls swooping and squawking. We passed a hill of dark green slime that had a sign that said YARD WASTE in front of it. Heaps of broken furniture, mounds of bottles and colored glass, and even last year's Christmas trees, brown and brittle, were everywhere.

As the bus stopped in front of a large cement building, Ashley's voice broke the stunned silence. "This is the *dump!*" she screeched. "Mrs. Barbage, the driver must have made a mistake. We're in the Westford dump."

"That's right," Mrs. Barbage said, standing in front of us. "Except that we don't call it a dump anymore. It's a landfill. And my husband is the landfill curator."

"It's still the dump," Ashley muttered.

"This isn't fair," Iggy said. "You told us we were going to an archaeological dig. You didn't say anything about the dump."

"Just be patient," Mrs. Barbage said, smiling her cat-like smile. "We have to wait here a few minutes for my husband. He's going to personally escort us on a tour of the landfill."

"Big deal," Iggy said, slumping down in his seat.

As we waited, Michael leaned over to us and whispered, "Can't you just see him?"

"Who?" I asked.

"Mr. Barbage, the dump manager. I'll bet he's a big fat porky guy with a belly so big he can't get through the door of the bus."

"You're right," I said and laughed. "Because he has to eat everything his wife cooks. She doesn't let him throw anything away because they don't own a garbage can."

"Yeah," Michael said, enjoying himself. "And flies buzz around his head all the time."

"And he has banana peels in his pocket—"

"And food stains all over his clothes," Peter added. "And he wears a shirt that's embroidered in red, 'Mr. Barbage, Director of Garbage.' "

"And he smells—really, really bad. He smells just like . . . just like . . ." I was trying to come up with the grossest smell I could think of.

Peter laughed. "Just like your Final Four sweatshirt

does when you get too close to it." He sniffed near my shoulder.

I stopped laughing. "It doesn't smell anymore. Mom got the stink all out."

"Not quite," Peter said. "Maybe you don't smell it, but it's still there."

I was about to get into a major argument with him when the bus door opened and a man in a three-piece suit came in. He was lean and trim with a little gray in his hair. He looked like a New York executive, and the bus was suddenly quiet again.

He put his arm around Mrs. Barbage and kissed her lightly on the forehead. She blushed. This was obviously Mr. Barbage. And he definitely did not look like a pigpen.

"What a hunk," I heard Ashley say to Steffie, and I suddenly felt a little twinge of jealousy.

Mr. Barbage introduced himself and said, "Welcome to the Westford Landfill."

But before he could say anything else, Iggy interrupted. "This stinks!" he said. "Mrs. Barbage said we were going to see archaeologists at work."

"And that's exactly what you will see," he said in his deep, rolling voice. "The Westford Landfill has been chosen by a team of archaeologists as a temporary dig. It's being run by the Garbage Gang, scientists who believe that the history of garbage is the history of civilization. I'm a project assistant, and it's amazing what I've been learning. Did you know, for example, that every man, woman, and child in the USA produces about four pounds of garbage a day? The garbage we produce in just one year, loaded onto large garbage trucks, would reach halfway to the moon.''

Iggy let out a low whistle, and Steffie said, ''Wow, that's a *lot* of garbage!''

Mr. Barbage nodded. ''But enough talk. Let's go exploring. Just stay together as a group; we wouldn't want to lose anyone along the way.''

As I got off the bus, I was hit in the face by a smell that was so overpowering I almost gagged. Jen and Sue were holding their noses. Mr. Barbage looked at all of us and laughed. ''You may notice a slight odor,'' he said. ''Dumps burp as they digest our garbage, releasing gas. I'm afraid rotting garbage will always smell. But you'll get used to it.''

We walked for a while, and then he stopped in front of a huge dirt mountain. A couple of old tires lay on it. ''For many years,'' he said, ''people just dug a big hole and dumped all their garbage in that. They assumed it would decompose and disappear, but we find that much of it is actually very well preserved because it's so tightly packed and exposed to little light or moisture. That's what we used to do here, before we became a sanitary landfill.''

''What's that?'' Michael asked.

''Instead of leaving a big open pit, every night we bulldoze earth over the trash, covering it. It keeps out rats and other animals, but there are still problems. Toxic chemicals, for example—half-empty cans of paint and turpentine, motor oil, dead batteries, and even half-full bottles of nail polish and cans of hair spray. Rainwater can filter through these chemicals and seep into the ground, contaminating drinking water. It's called *leaching*."

"That's gross," Ed said. "Do you mean there's gunk in our water? I'm drinking nothing but Coke from now on."

"Our water in Westford is being constantly tested, and it's still safe," he said. "But we want to keep it that way. Now follow me to the top of this hill. I want to show you something."

When we got to the top, two big garbage trucks went rumbling by, and the ground beneath us started to wiggle. It was like standing on a giant bowl of Jell-O. "We're standing on a mountain of garbage," Mr. Barbage said. "And you see those tires? As trucks pass over the landfill, they work their way to the surface, like noodles in a boiling pot of soup. Every week new ones pop up. But come on. Let's keep exploring."

We walked farther along until Mr. Barbage stopped in front of an area with heavy machinery and a lot of people digging around by hand. "What we're doing here is digging up thousands of pounds of garbage, weighing every item we find, and sorting them into twenty-seven different categories. It is, actually, an archaeological dig. After our study, we hope to come up with some solutions to the problems associated with garbage."

Iggy frowned. "I still don't think you're really archaeologists," he said.

I thought Iggy was being kind of rude, but I had to agree with him.

Mr. Barbage smiled. "I know what you mean," he

64

said. "But think about it. All archaeologists study garbage. Ours is just a little fresher. We use a machine that works a lot like a giant cookie cutter, cutting through layers of garbage and lifting them up. It reaches down as far as a hundred feet."

He pulled on a pair of heavy gloves, reached into a storage bin, and held up a bottle. "Here, let me give you an example. What do you think this is?"

Ed snorted. "It's a Coke bottle," he said. "Anyone knows that."

Mr. Barbage smiled. "Exactly correct," he said. "But this particular Coke bottle dates back to 1955." Then he held up something that looked like an old head of lettuce and an ear of corn. "And this ear of corn, even though it's a little dry, dates back to 1972, and the lettuce is from 1984. One of the most common foods we find are hot dogs. Here's one that someone threw out in 1966. I guess their preservatives do work," he added with a chuckle.

"I don't get it," Iggy said. "There are no dates on hot dogs or corn. How do you know how old that stuff is?"

Mr. Barbage put back the hot dog and said, "When we dig down through the layers of garbage, we can date all the items by the newspapers we find in the same layer. They don't decompose as quickly as people once thought. Look at this." He showed us a newspaper that looked brand-new, but the date on it was August 29, 1978.

He reached back into the bin and pulled out something else. "People have a lot of mistaken ideas about garbage," he said. "Take this disposable diaper, for ex-

65

ample. It's estimated to be around eleven or twelve years old." He stopped talking for a second, looked at the diaper he was holding, and then at us. "Come to think of it, one of you might have worn this very diaper. Most of you wore disposables, right?"

I didn't even want to think about it. A couple of the girls were giggling and blushing. Most of the boys were just looking at the ground.

"Anyway," Mr. Barbage continued, "a lot of people think that disposable diapers and plastic bags and fast-food Styrofoam containers are taking up most of our landfill space. But they're wrong. Out of the four thousand pounds of garbage that we've weighed and sorted, there were only two pounds of fast-food packaging, and less than four pounds of disposable diapers. The real problem in landfills is plain old paper, especially newspapers and telephone books. Almost half of everything we throw away is paper."

Our last stop on the tour was Mr. Barbage's office. Even though it was clean and tidy, nothing matched, and some of the furniture seemed to be made of old piping and apple crates. "My office is a recycler's paradise," he said. "Everything you see in here is something that someone no longer had any use for."

Peter, Michael, and I were looking at some pictures on the wall. "These didn't come from the dump," I whispered. There was a picture of Mr. Barbage shaking hands with the President of the United States. Underneath was a framed letter of commendation signed by the governor. Pretty impressive.

By the time our bus came, we were almost sorry to leave. "Just remember," Mr. Barbage said as we boarded the bus, "the next time you throw something away, think twice. It might have another use."

Even though I had gotten used to the smell, my stomach was feeling a little queasy. Mrs. Barbage turned to Iggy and asked, "Did you still want to have your picnic lunch down by the dig, Iggy?"

"No, thanks, Mrs. B. I'll pass."

CHAPTER TWELVE

Everybody on the bus was talking about garbage. "Can you believe the stuff people throw away?" I asked Peter and Michael.

"Unbelievable. I'm going to pay a lot more attention to what goes into the garbage can at home," Peter said. "Otherwise, twenty years from now, garbage could move us right off our planet."

"I never thought much about garbage," Michael added. "But I sure do have a lot more respect for it."

Mrs. Barbage was looking extremely pleased. "I'm proud of all of you," she said. "I've arranged to have our picnic at The Sundae School—I'm sure most of you know the place. And after lunch, ice cream for everyone—my treat!"

We all gave a cheer for Mrs. Barbage.

As we piled off the bus and ran for the picnic area, I looked around for my old friend Wobbles. But he wasn't with the other ducks down by the pond. In fact, there didn't seem to be as many ducks as there usually were. Oh, well, maybe they were off sleeping somewhere.

I hadn't been to The Sundae School for a couple of weeks, and somehow the place looked different. Bits of paper, plastic bags, old soda cans, cigarette butts, and a couple of empty tuna fish cans littered the area. We wiped off the picnic tables as best we could, but they looked dirty and run-down.

"How come this place is such a mess?" Ashley asked. She picked up a plastic bag that had a half-eaten sandwich in it. Holding it up between her thumb and first finger, she looked around. "Where's a garbage can?" And when she couldn't find one, she dropped the plastic sandwich bag on the ground.

"This used to be a nice place," Peter said. "Now it looks worse than a dump. I wonder why."

"People," Mrs. Barbage said. "People have no idea what they're doing to the environment."

"But The Sundae School's only been open a couple of weeks," I said.

"It doesn't take much time to make a mess," she answered. "But come on, let's do what we can to make our lunch area a little nicer. I brought along a couple of big black garbage bags. Let's throw some of the stuff that's around in one of them."

"I'm not picking up other people's garbage," Ashley said, and she sat down on one of the picnic benches. But when she saw everyone else, even the girls, working, she got up and started to help.

It only took about ten minutes to get our picnic area cleaned up. After we washed our hands, Mrs. Barbage spread yellow tablecloths on two of the tables, and we unpacked our lunches and started to eat. A couple of ducks waddled over to us, and we threw bits of our sandwiches to them.

"When you're finished with your lunch," Mrs. Barbage said, "go inside and order an ice-cream sundae. They're all paid for. But be sure to gather up all your trash and put it into the garbage bag. Since there don't seem to be any garbage cans around, I'll take all of our trash back to school and dispose of it properly."

"Come on, Murphy," Peter said when we were finished eating. "I could go for a big fat ice-cream sundae."

"You go ahead. I'll be right in," I said. "I want to look for someone."

Michael laughed. "Ashley? She's right over there, talking to Steffie."

"Don't start," I said.

"Then who do you want to look for?"

I started to walk toward the pond with Peter and Michael following. "You'll probably laugh at me," I said. "But I want to find Wobbles."

"That big fat duck that's always around here?" Peter asked. "The one we always feed when we come? I didn't know he had a name."

"A friend of mine named him," I answered. A used-to-be friend, I thought. "I didn't see him with the other ducks, and I was just wondering if he was around someplace."

"We'll help you find him," Peter said. "Then we can go get our ice cream."

We walked down toward the pond where some of the ducks were lying around, sleeping with their bills tucked

70

behind one wing. A couple seemed to be asleep standing on one foot, which made them look like one-legged ducks. The pond, which had been crystal clear a few weeks ago, looked scummy, and Styrofoam cups and bits of paper floated in the water.

I spotted Wobbles off by himself, down by the edge of the pond. At first I almost didn't recognize him. His feathers had lost their brilliant shine, his eyes looked cloudy, and he had lost some weight. But when he came toward me, I recognized Wobbles' funny, wobbly walk.

"There he is," I called.

"What's the matter with him?" Peter asked.

"I don't know. Do you have anything left to eat? Maybe he's hungry."

Michael fished into his jacket pocket and pulled out a small bag of popcorn. "I was saving it for the bus trip home. But you can have it."

Wobbles had taken a few steps and then stopped. He looked tired. And, if I didn't know better, I'd say he looked sad. I held a couple of pieces of the popcorn in my hand, but he still didn't move. I went over to him and dropped the popcorn right in front of him. Still nothing. He just sat there, not moving, looking sick.

"Something's wrong with him," Peter said.

"Let's find Farmer Brown," I said. "Maybe he knows."

Farmer Brown was near the picnic tables talking to Mrs. Barbage. We rushed over to them. I didn't mean to be rude and I didn't mean to interrupt their conversation, but I did. "What's wrong with Wobbles?" I asked. When Farmer Brown looked confused, I added, "The

71

duck—the big fat one. He's down by the pond, and I think he's sick.''

He shook his head sadly. "A lot of the ducks are sick,'' he said. "A couple of them have died.''

Ashley and Steffie and some of the other kids had gathered around. Even Iggy seemed to be interested.

"Why are they dying?'' Iggy asked. "Is someone shooting them? Or poisoning them?''

"No,'' Farmer Brown answered. "No guns and no poison. Just garbage. The ducks are scavengers. They eat all the little bits of food that people drop on the ground.''

"And you want us to believe that kills them?'' I asked. Obviously Farmer Brown wasn't too smart.

"It's not the food,'' he said. "It's the litter—the cigarette butts, the pieces of Styrofoam. And lots of times people drop sandwich bags that have food left inside. The ducks go after the food and gobble up bits of plastic bag with the food. The plastic gets stuck in their throats and suffocates them. It's a terrible problem.''

I looked at Iggy, remembering the plastic bag he had left on the ground when he was at The Sundae School teasing me. But Iggy was looking at the ground, so I guess he didn't care.

"There are other problems,'' Farmer Brown continued. "When people leave half-open cans of food around, especially those snack-food cans with the peel-off aluminum tops, raccoons and squirrels and chipmunks go after what's left in them. Then they get themselves stuck or get cut on the razor-sharp tops. And we've had ducks get caught in the plastic rings that hold six-packs

72

of soda together. When they dive into the water looking for food, they can get tangled in the rings and drown, strangle, or starve.''

I was listening, but I was getting madder and madder at Farmer Brown. "Then why do you leave this place such a mess?" I finally asked. "There are no garbage cans around, and the place looks like the dump—worse than the dump.''

"I just can't keep up with it," he said. "And this year seems especially bad. We have quite a few acres of meadows and ponds and forests that we've tried to keep as a sanctuary for ducks and birds, but it's just too much for me and my family to keep clean. And as for garbage cans—we had them, but they get beat up and vandalized. We bought new ones at the beginning of the year, but they disappeared. I guess someone walked off with them.''

"So what are you going to do?" Peter asked. "You can't keep letting the animals die.''

"It's gotten so that it costs too much money to keep the place going," he said. "I've had a call from a developer who wants to buy the property. I hate to do it, but I've been thinking about selling. He wants to put up condominiums.''

"But what about the animals?" Ashley asked. "What will happen to them?''

"I don't know," he said. "I have about a month to decide what to do. That's when I have a meeting with the developer." He shook hands with Mrs. Barbage. "You have a nice bunch of kids here—and neat, too. Enjoy the rest of your day.''

"Did you all get your ice cream?" Mrs. Barbage asked.

"We almost forgot," Peter said to Michael and me. "You feel like getting that sundae?"

I thought about it for a minute. "Nah, I'm not much in the mood for ice cream."

"Me, neither," Peter said as Michael shook his head.

CHAPTER THIRTEEN

Isn't there *anything* we can do, Mrs. Barbage?" Ashley asked. "I love that farm. There must be *something* we can do."

We were in cooking class, and Mrs. Barbage had done a follow-up lesson on our trip to the dump. And while everyone was glad that Westford's dump was being modernized, we were all concerned about the farm. At least, most of us were.

"Don't be stupid, Ashley," Ed said. "We're just kids. And kids can't save that farm."

"I'll bet we could," I said. "I think if we put some effort into it, maybe we could save the farm."

Ed turned to me. "Sticking up for your girlfriend, Murphy?"

"Shut up, Ed. I'm talking about the farm. And those animals. Somebody has to do something. And since the adults don't seem to care much, maybe we should. Even if we are only kids."

Ed turned to Iggy, looking for support, but Iggy was deep in thought, picking at his fingernails.

Mrs. Barbage clapped her hands and brought us all to order. "I've been doing a lot of thinking about the problem," she said. "I wasn't sure you'd be interested, but since you brought it up this morning, I think we should try to think of a way to help."

"We could raise money," Steffie said. "Money to buy garbage cans."

"And maybe some money to bring in a doctor to look at the sick animals," Michael added.

"And more money to hire people to clean up the garbage," Jen said.

"That sounds like an awful lot of money," Mrs. Barbage said. "But I like the idea of raising money for garbage cans."

"But what will keep people from stealing them again?" Ashley asked.

"Maybe we could buy chains and chain them to the trees, or to the fence," I suggested.

"Good idea," Peter said.

I turned to Ashley and smiled. I loved getting ideas that solved problems, especially problems she brought up.

"Okay," Mrs. Barbage said. "That's decided. I think we could probably raise enough money to buy garbage cans. Let's brainstorm some ideas for fund-raisers."

"How about a car wash?" I suggested. "We could charge four dollars a car and make lots of money."

"We're supposed to be into saving the environment," Ashley said, looking smug. "A car wash would waste a lot of water."

76

"It was just an idea," I said. "That's what brainstorming is all about. At least I came up with something."

We all went back to thinking. "I've got it," Ashley squealed. She stood up and faced the class. "A balloon sale. Kids buy a balloon for a dollar, tie their name and address on them, and maybe even a message about saving the environment. Then we have a gigantic balloon launch. I can see it now—hundreds of colored helium balloons floating in the air. And when they land, whoever finds them will read the messages and write back." She stopped talking and folded her arms, looking like she was waiting for applause.

"It sounds like a wonderful idea, Ashley," Mrs. Barbage said. "But there is a problem. When helium balloons are released, they can blow into the ocean, even if it's hundreds of miles away. The salt water washes off the color, and sea creatures think they're food and eat them. Sea turtles, for example, mistake balloons for jellyfish—which look and wiggle just like them. The balloon blocks their stomach, and they can starve to death."

Ashley sat down, looking like a deflated balloon. I was going to make a sarcastic remark to her, but she looked put down enough.

"How about a Trash-a-Thon?" I said. "My mother was in a Walk-a-Thon a few weeks ago to raise money. She got pledges from people who promised to pay for every mile she walked. Some people pledged a dollar, some pledged five dollars, and some only twenty-five cents. Whatever they felt they could afford. But Mom raised quite a bit of money for charity."

"So what's a Trash-a-Thon?" Ashley asked. "A long walk through the dump?" Everybody laughed.

I ignored her sarcasm. "We get pledges for collecting bags of garbage around town," I said. "There has to be enough litter around to make quite a bit of money."

"But what about all the trash and litter that's at The Sundae School?" Steffie asked. "Do you think we can raise money to hire people to clean the place up?"

Suddenly Ashley came alive again. "I have an even better idea," she said. "We can collect all the garbage that's around The Sundae School. People make pledges, and we clean up the farm. We'll call our campaign Adopt-a-Farm. We'll be cleaning up the farm and raising money for the garbage cans at the same time. Isn't that the best idea yet?"

Everyone was getting all excited. And everyone was congratulating Ashley on her great idea. "Let's not forget who thought up the Trash-a-Thon idea!" I shouted. But I wasn't sure if anyone heard me. Oh, well, as long as we save the farm, I thought.

Suddenly Ed spoke up. "I'm not wasting my time cleaning up anybody else's garbage. You can just count me out. I've got better things to do than worry about a place that's for kids—and lovers." And he shot me a look.

"That's strictly up to you, Ed," Mrs. Barbage said. "No one is required to participate. Let's have a show of hands. How many of you would like to adopt the farm and work on a Trash-a-Thon?"

Everyone's hand—except for Ed's—went up. Iggy started to raise his, but when he saw the puzzled look Ed was giving him, he put it back down.

78

"Iggy?" Mrs. Barbage asked. "Are you in or out?"
He looked at Mrs. Barbage, then at Ed, then back at
Mrs. Barbage. "Out," he said quietly.

"That means there are only eight of you. Do you
think it's enough?" Mrs. Barbage asked.

"I'll bet a lot of the other kids in our class would
help," I said. "I'll ask them later and get whoever's
interested to sign up."

Mrs. Barbage smiled. "I like your enthusiasm, Murphy," she said. "Since the Trash-a-Thon was your idea,
I'm going to put you in charge."

Ashley looked mad and started to wave her hand in
the air, trying to get Mrs. Barbage's attention.

Mrs. Barbage turned to her. "And since the Adopt-
a-Farm project was *your* idea, Ashley, you are also in
charge. You and Murphy will work together. And I do
hope you *will* work together. This is too important to
allow personal disagreements to stand in the way."

Ashley and I just glared at each other.

"Now, in the meantime," Mrs. Barbage said, "on to
bread."

We all looked at her, puzzled. Sometimes she reminded me of Iggy because she talked in phrases. But
she was an awful lot nicer than Iggy.

"We've done a lot of different projects, and our next
one will be bread. Each team will have to decide what
level of difficulty to choose when selecting a bread to
bake—easy, medium, or hard. The easy and the medium categories consist of quick breads, breads that
don't have yeast in the ingredients. I have recipes for
muffins or biscuits that are super-easy. Then there's
banana-nut bread, corn bread, and cranberry bread in

79

the medium category. The hard breads are the yeast breads. These require time, patience, and ability. I recommend this category only for those of you who feel confident in the kitchen."

She handed each of us a booklet of recipes. "Look them over together," she said, "and I'll be coming around to each kitchen to write down your choice."

Ashley and I sat at our table, looking over the different recipes. "Let's go for easy or medium," I suggested. When she didn't answer me, I added, "That way you can't mess it up."

"Me?" she practically screamed. "Every disaster we've had has been your fault. Look at what you did to the rice. And look what happened when you rigged the sprayer. We haven't done one really great thing yet. Now you want to do easy bread because you're a loser in the kitchen."

"Who are you calling a loser, loser? I just know how much trouble you have boiling water. But okay, we'll do a medium bread."

"Think you can handle it?" she asked. "You might have to use eggs. And every time you break an egg, shell gets into the bowl. Then you have to go sticking your dirty fingers in the bowl to fish it out. You just think I don't notice."

"Oh, yeah?" I said. "Well, for your information, if I had a halfway decent partner, I know I could do the hard bread."

"And if my partner was anything other than a lower form of life, I could breeze through a hard bread. In fact, I could do it alone."

We were almost ready to start throwing punches

when Mrs. Barbage came over with her book. Pen poised, she asked sweetly, "And your decision?"

I glared at Ashley. Sparks were practically coming out of her eyes. Without taking our eyes off each other, we both took a deep breath. *"Hard,"* we said, almost at the same time.

I pulled my eyes away from Ashley and looked at Mrs. Barbage. She was smiling. "Are you quite sure?" she asked. "It's going to take a lot of cooperation. And for this project you'll have to read directions carefully and work on your own as much as you can."

I wasn't going to back down and neither was Ashley. "Yes," we both said. "We're sure."

CHAPTER FOURTEEN

The next day as we were walking to cooking class, I asked Peter, "What are you and Aggie making—white bread or whole wheat?"

"Neither," he said. "We're doing a medium bread. I think Aggie chose the banana-nut recipe. She says yeast breads are too much trouble. And I agree. Banana-nut is enough of a challenge for me."

"For *you?*" I stopped and looked at him. "Who are you kidding? You haven't cooked one thing yet. Aggie does it all, and you're getting an A-plus."

"Sounds to me like you're a little jealous," he said. "You should have picked your partner more carefully."

"I didn't exactly pick her. I wanted you to be my partner, remember?"

He just smiled. "And pass up a chance for an automatic A? Are you kidding? Besides, I set the table and help clean up," he said as he walked over to his kitchen.

"Big deal."

Ashley wasn't in class yet, so I sat down at our table to read the recipe. Attached to it was a two-page explanation about yeast breads—long, detailed instructions in small print. Mrs. Barbage had told us to take it home and study it, but I had forgotten all about it.

I didn't want to start alone, so I folded up the recipe and waited. After a few minutes I began to wonder where she was. Maybe she wasn't coming. Maybe she went home sick or something. Maybe then I could tell Mrs. Barbage we decided to do an easy bread, like muffins, instead.

As I was about to talk to Mrs. Barbage, Ashley walked in with a note for being late. So I went back to reading the recipe:

Perfect White Bread

1 package active dry yeast
3½ cups all-purpose flour
1¼ cups milk
1 tablespoon sugar
1 tablespoon shortening
1 teaspoon salt

When Ashley finally came over, I asked, "Did you read through the recipe last night? It's got two pages of 'Helpful Hints' attached to it."

"No," she said. "I had too much other homework."

"Then we'd better read this through carefully first,

especially these two long pages—so we know what we're doing.''

"We don't have time," she said. "I had to call my mother about something. That's why I was late for class. Let's get started."

"But it looks really complicated. Don't you think we should—"

"I think you should stop talking and get to work. We'll just follow the recipe step-by-step. Help me get the stuff together."

When we had collected all of the ingredients, Ashley said, "Read me the directions. I'll be in charge of the mixing."

"Suit yourself," I said. I stood next to her, holding the recipe. " 'In a large mixing bowl combine the yeast and two cups of flour.' "

She opened a canister marked YEAST. "How much?" she asked.

"I don't know. It says one package."

"This isn't a package," she said. "It's a whole can."

"Let's ask Mrs. Barbage," I said.

"Let's not. We'll get a better grade if we figure it out by ourselves. I'm going to put in a cup. That should be enough."

"How do you know?" I asked.

"Female intuition. Don't argue with me," she said, dumping the yeast into the bowl. "What's next?"

"Flour."

She started to measure out the flour when she turned to me and said, "Don't just stand there watching me. Do something useful. Start the next step."

Thoughts of dumping the flour over her head crossed

my mind, but I could see Mrs. Barbage at her desk, and she had a clear view of me. I read the next step in the recipe: " 'In saucepan heat milk, sugar, shortening, and salt just till warm, stirring *constantly* till shortening almost melts.' "

I banged a saucepan onto the stove, measured out the milk, margarine, and salt, turned the heat up, and started stirring. At the last minute I realized that I didn't put in the sugar, and I couldn't remember how much. The recipe was next to Ashley, who was still measuring and mixing.

"How much sugar?" I shouted over to her.

She kept mixing.

"Hey, Ashley. How much sugar does the recipe call for?"

"I don't know," she yelled back. "Come over and look. That's part of *your* job."

What a pain. I didn't want to stop stirring, and I couldn't see the recipe from where I was, so I dumped in half a cup. The sugar made it kind of gloppy, so I added a little more margarine and made a nice pasty mixture.

"I'm done," Ashley called. "What's next?"

I carried the saucepan to the recipe and read, " 'Add to dry mixture and beat with electric mixer for one-half minute, scraping sides of bowl constantly.' "

She turned the mixer on high and stuck it in the bowl. The flour and the yeast puffed up in her face.

She turned off the mixer, grabbed a towel, and wiped her face. A white dab was left on the tip of her nose, and I laughed.

"What are you laughing at?" she asked. She looked hurt, and for a minute I thought she might cry.

"Nothing," I said, reaching for a towel. "You still have flour on your nose. Hold still," and I took the towel and wiped it off.

She looked at me strangely, started to open her mouth to say something, and then smiled at me. "Thanks," she said.

When the recipe said, "Knead the dough till smooth and elastic, about ten minutes," I had to check the "Helpful Hints" to see what "kneading" meant. Basically, we had to punch and roll and shove the dough around with our hands.

"Sounds like fun," I said, but the dough was all loose and icky, and after a few minutes my hands and fingers got cramped, so I passed the dough to Ashley.

She dipped her hands in flour, shoved the dough around for the next couple of minutes, and then, when she got tired, I took over again. By the time we had each done three turns at kneading, the dough was as smooth and tight as a gigantic, well-chewed ball of gum.

Ashley and I were covered with enough flour to bake three breads, and we were tired. But we weren't fighting anymore. We stood there, looking at the pale lump of dough that had caused us so much trouble.

"It sure doesn't look like much," I finally said. "I'll bet if we flattened it out it would be about the size of a slice of bread. Maybe we did something wrong."

Ashley shook her head. "No, I think it has to rise. That's why we put yeast in it. It's supposed to get bigger."

"When?"

"I don't know. Read the rest of the recipe."

I flattened out the recipe. It was so covered with grease, flour, and some mysterious brown spots, that I had a hard time reading it. "It says, 'Place dough in a lightly greased bowl. Cover; let rise in warm (eighty degrees) place till double in size, usually a few hours (the warmth helps the dough to rise). Punch dough down. Dough can be refrigerated at this point and finished the next day.' "

I looked at Ashley. "The rest of the directions tell what we're supposed to do tomorrow."

Ashley groaned. "That means we'll have to come back this afternoon."

"Just to punch the dough down," I said. "You could probably do it by yourself in ten minutes flat."

"Me? You want me to come back here by myself to punch bread?"

"No," I said. "You're right. I'll come, too."

There went my afternoon of baseball with the guys. Oh, well, how long could it take to knock out some old dough?

"There's another problem," Ashley said.

"Now what?"

"It doesn't say exactly how long it'll take the dough to rise. Who knows, we could be waiting around for that dough to do its thing until four o'clock this afternoon."

Just what I always wanted to do—wait around for a lump of dough to get fat. Then my brain got a spectacular idea. Sometimes I even amazed myself. "Ashley, see how the recipe says the warmth helps the dough rise? I'll set the oven on warm, two hundred degrees, and put the bowl with the dough on top of it. Since it's twice as warm, it should grow twice as fast. Then we'll come back right after school, punch it down, stick it in the refrigerator, and finish it tomorrow."

"I don't think it'll work."

"Sure it will. Trust me. There's no reason for us to hang around baby-sitting our dough." I turned the oven on. "It'll taste terrific, Ashley. You'll see." I put the dough on the warm stove. "Sleep tight, little lump," I said, giving it a pat and covering it with a clean dishtowel. "Just think, in a couple of hours you'll be all grown up into a big fat lump."

"I sure hope so," Ashley said. "With our luck, he'll stay small and ugly for the rest of his life."

"No, he won't," I assured her.

We cleaned up our kitchen together, and it felt pretty good not to be enemies anymore. Mrs. Barbage was right. When people work together making something and it turns out right, it's a great feeling.

CHAPTER FIFTEEN

Right after school Ashley and I headed for the home economics room. The door was locked, and then we remembered our special passes. It took us a while to find the custodian, and even longer to convince him that he had to let us in the room right away.

"I'm kind of busy," he said. It looked to me like he was just leaning on his broom, waiting for the halls to clear out.

"It won't take us long," Ashley said. "All you have to do is let us in. You can leave the door locked. We'll make sure it's shut when we leave."

He grumbled a little but followed us to the room. By the time he unlocked the door, the halls were almost empty. No one wanted to hang around longer than they had to.

"I hope the lump grew enough," I said to Ashley as I closed the door.

Suddenly I heard Ashley scream. I wheeled around.

Our little lump of dough had transformed itself into something resembling a second cousin of The Blob. It had grown enormous, oozing over the edge of the bowl, dripping down the stove, and ending in a swelling puddle on the floor.

Even as we watched, it seemed to heave and sigh. A large bubble slowly puffed up and erupted. Another lump plopped onto the floor. It was growing in front of our eyes.

The smell was awful—like a moldy swamp on a wet day.

"What happened?" Ashley gasped.

"Something went wrong," I said.

She turned and glared at me. "No kidding! This is all your fault, Murphy Darinzo. You must have read the directions wrong."

I was shocked. "*My* fault? You're blaming *me?* I was the one who wanted to read those two pages of helpful hints first. And I was the one who said we should ask Mrs. Barbage for help. But oh, no, not you, not Ms. Independent who said we could figure it all out by ourselves."

"And we could have, if you had half a brain!"

So much for the good feelings about making bread together.

"What are we going to do?" Ashley finally asked.

"Maybe it just needs punching down. Maybe the lump just got carried away and needs to be disciplined. Try punching it down."

"I'm not touching that stuff. It'll probably suck my whole hand in, and then my arm, and then I'll be gone."

That would take care of one of my problems, I

thought. "Don't you think you're exaggerating a little, Ashley? It's just bread dough, not some alien from outer space."

But she looked as if she wasn't quite sure. And every time another bubble belched or another clump dropped to the floor, Ashley took another step backward.

"We'll have to get rid of it," I said.

"How?" she asked. "We can't throw it into the garbage. You know how Mrs. Barbage gets about throwing food away. Besides, if we leave it here overnight, it might devour the whole room by morning. It's still growing."

"We'll have to smuggle it out of the room. Get it out of school. Then figure a way to get rid of it."

"I'm not touching it!"

"Don't be such a baby, Ashley. It's just dough."

"But it's disgusting. And it smells." She wrinkled up her nose. "Maybe the yeast was no good."

"Stop making excuses," I said. "Let's just clean it up and get it out of here."

We looked around the classroom for something to put the dough in. But there was nothing—no plastic bags, no paper bags, and no container big enough to get it all in.

"How about dumping it out the window," Ashley suggested.

I looked out and saw a couple of custodians raking the lawn. "No. We'll have to carry it out in something." I kept walking around the room, looking for something, anything to put it in. "Our book bags," I finally said. "We'll have to get it out of here in our book bags."

"I have books and papers in mine," she said.

"So take them out and carry them."

"I'm *not* putting that sticky glop in my bag."

"You have a better idea?"

She looked again at the growing dough. "No. But we'd better hurry before it gets too big for both our bags."

We unzipped and emptied our book bags and walked toward the heaving mass. Slowly I reached out and tried to scoop up some that had fallen on the floor. It felt like warm rubber cement. As I handled the blob, it started to collapse. I shoved it in my bag, working hard to make it let go of my fingers.

Ashley was standing there, watching.

"Come on, Ashley. Help. Get the stuff that's on the stove. Try punching it down first. It seems to shrink when you touch it."

She reached her hand toward the bowl and softly patted the dough. Nothing happened, except that it got stuck on her hand. She patted harder, and her hand disappeared in the mass. "It's got my hand!" she squealed.

I had shoved all of the dough from the floor in my book bag and stood up to help Ashley. "Just be firm with it. You have to show it who's boss. Pull your hand out and open your book bag."

Her hand came out of the middle of the bowl with a big *thwock*, and the lump of dough started to shrink. The more we handled it, the smaller it got. After about ten minutes all the dough had been stuffed into both our bags. We washed off whatever was left on the stove

92

and the floor, washed the rest of the sticky goo off our hands, and left.

We were carrying our bags in one hand and our books in the other when Ashley spotted Mrs. Barbage coming down the hall. We looked for an open classroom to duck into, but it was too late.

"Hi, kids," she said. "I knew you'd be here. I wondered if you needed any help."

I smiled. "No, we're just fine."

"How's the yeast bread coming? It's a tricky project. Yeast is usually sold in small packages, but I bought it in bulk. That's why I put the conversion directions in the explanation. If you put in too much yeast or too much sugar, all sorts of things can go wrong."

Now you tell us, I thought. "It's fine," I said. "Really."

"Can I take a look at it?" she asked.

Suddenly I felt Ashley poke me in the back. I started to turn toward her, but then I noticed my book bag. The dough was starting to squeeze up through the zipper. I looked at Ashley, who was holding her book bag behind her back.

Ashley started to talk double-time. "We'd love to show you, Mrs. B., but we want the bread to be a surprise. I know this is going to be the best bread you've ever seen. And we have so much homework to do, we have to rush home now."

She smiled at us. "You must have an awful lot," she said. "You each have an armful of books and your book bags looked jammed. What do you have in them?"

I could almost feel my book bag puffing out bigger and bigger behind me. I had visions of a gigantic explosion and yeast dough covering all of us. "It's . . . ah . . . stuff for a project." I gave my bag a kick, hoping the dough would shrink down again. "We really have to get going," I said, bumping Ashley.

We kept our bags behind us and walked slowly by Mrs. Barbage, facing her the whole time. "Promise us you won't look at our dough," Ashley called when we were about ten feet away from her. "We want it to be a surprise." And we turned and ran out of the building as fast as we could.

A few blocks from school we stopped running and put our bags down. The dough was squishing out between the zippers. "What are we going to do?" I asked.

"With the dough? I'm going to find a big garbage can somewhere and get rid of it. Or else bury it somewhere."

"Not the dough," I said. "What are we going to do about the bread? We're supposed to bake it tomorrow. We're going to end up with a zero. Unless you can get your mother to make some new dough tonight."

"My mother? My mother doesn't bake. She hardly even cooks. She works full-time."

"I know," I said. "But I heard my mother say that your mother bakes the best homemade bread. That was last weekend, when my parents went to your house for that dinner party."

Ashley just laughed. "She doesn't bake. She buys it frozen in the supermarket, defrosts it, and sticks it in the oven."

My mouth fell open. "And then she tells everyone she baked it?"

"No, she doesn't. She doesn't say anything. I guess everyone thinks she's a great cook because she wears a fancy apron when she's serving dinner. Most of the food comes from a caterer or from the supermarket frozen and—"

Ashley stopped talking and looked at me. "How much money do you have?" she asked.

"I don't know. A dollar and some change. Why?"

"Because, stupid. We can buy frozen bread, just like my mother does, and bake it in class tomorrow."

"That's dishonest," I said.

"Would you rather get a zero?"

I thought for a minute. "Not really."

"Then give me your money. I'll buy the dough, and we'll both get an A-plus. Guaranteed."

"I still think it's dishonest," I said. But when I saw the dough bulging out of my bag, I reached in my pocket and handed over $1.37.

CHAPTER SIXTEEN

Our bread was a masterpiece. Ashley had bought it and then defrosted it in her room overnight, and I had sneaked it into the cooking room refrigerator early in the morning. We poked around with it a little, then put it on a baking sheet and stuck it in the preheated oven. After a half hour we had the most delicious-smelling browned loaf of bread I had ever seen.

When Mrs. Barbage came over with her grade book, even she seemed a little surprised. "My, my, my— isn't that a professional-looking loaf of bread." I thought she sounded suspicious but decided it was my imagination.

"That's because we worked together, Mrs. Barbage," Ashley said sweetly. She cut two big slices, buttered them, put them on plates, and handed one to me. "Would you like to taste it, Mrs. Barbage?" she asked.

But Mrs. Barbage had stopped paying attention. She kept picking up her left foot, like she was doing some odd dance. Then she reached down and took something off the sole of her shoe.

"Did you step in gum?" Ashley asked.

Mrs. Barbage was rolling a small gray lump in her fingers. "It doesn't feel like gum," she said. She sniffed it. "It smells almost like . . . yeast." She looked puzzled and put the lump in her apron pocket. Then she leaned over again. "There seems to be some of this same substance on your book bag, Murphy."

I could feel my cheeks start to burn. "It must be . . . uhh . . . I was doing papier-mâché for a science project and . . . uhh . . . it was kind of messy."

"Were you doing the same project, Ashley?" she asked as she took a piece of gray glop from Ashley's bag.

"Yes, Mrs. Barbage. I told you. Murphy and I have been working together. But never mind that. Taste our bread." And she offered Mrs. Barbage a slice.

"No, taste is for you and Murphy to decide. I'll grade you on the other areas of the project. And your bread certainly seems to be of bakery quality." There was that tone of suspicion again. I was beginning to think it wasn't my imagination.

We both took a bite. But my mouth was so dry that I was having trouble swallowing.

Mrs. Barbage watched and waited.

Ashley looked a little flushed. "I think it's worth an A," she said quietly. "Or maybe an A-minus."

I couldn't stand the guilty feeling in my stomach. "We should only get a B," I said. "It's a little soggy."

Ashley glared at me. "B-minus," she said, unwilling to be outdone.

That made me mad. "C," I said. "It's tough."

Ashley's jaws got tight and her eyes narrowed. "Oh, yeah?" she said, her mouth barely moving. "C-minus is more like it. Because *you* baked it too long. It tastes burned."

"Then make it a D because it was *your* dumb idea in the first place." I was practically shouting.

Suddenly we both realized that Mrs. Barbage was still standing there, her head jerking back and forth like she was watching a Ping-Pong match. "You've argued yourselves down to a D," she said. "Don't you think that's low enough?"

We both watched silently as she put a mark in her grade book and moved to another kitchen. Ashley picked another little lump of dough off the floor and threw it at me. I wondered if we'd ever get along.

With five minutes left in the class, Mrs. Barbage clapped her hands for attention. "Before you leave," she said, "I want to tell you what our next—and final—project is going to be. You've had six weeks of cooking, and I must say I'm pleased with what you've learned. Many of you have made mistakes, but you have all learned something from those mistakes."

You can say that again, I thought to myself.

She continued: "For our very last project, we're going to cook a five-course meal. I have written the names of the courses on slips of paper, put them in this box, and will let you draw. Whatever course you draw will be your responsibility. You can choose something from one of the cookbooks I have here. But you might like to create your own dish. We've done a lot of different things, and you may want to experiment. Anyway, let's start by drawing the courses.''

She held up a shoe box. Iggy drew first. "It says *entrée,*" he said. "What's that?''

Mrs. Barbage smiled. "That's a fancy way of saying 'main course.' You and Ed might consider cooking a casserole or a pasta dish. Okay, who's next?''

One by one we chose. Steffie and Michael got dessert. Peter and Aggie got appetizers. Sue and Jen picked salad. Ashley and I got soup.

"Now," said Mrs. Barbage, "since this is our last project, it will be the grand finale. And the grade that you get on your dish will be one of the most important grades of the whole course. You will be graded on the basis of nutritional value, cost to prepare, creativity of the name, and, as usual, your own grade for taste. I'll give you a week to look through recipe books and brainstorm, and a week from tomorrow we'll have the Great Westford Elementary Cook-off. Remember—try to create something special and original.''

Maybe Ashley and I still had a chance to pull our bread mark out of the hole we had talked it into. If I got a C in cooking, it would keep me off the honor roll.

"One more thing," Mrs. Barbage said. "How are we coming with our Adopt-a-Farm/Trash-a-Thon project? Murphy? Ashley?''

We hadn't even talked about it. "We've been working hard," I said.

"Could you give us a progress report Monday during class and let us know exactly what you're planning?'' she asked.

I looked at Ashley.

"Sure," she said. "Why not?"

After school Ashley called me aside. "We'd better do something about getting some kind of report together. Did you get any other kids to help?"

"A couple," I said. "I figured we'd work out the details over the weekend."

"I wrote down some ideas, and I also have some names," she said. She reached into her book bag and started looking for something. "Oh, yuck." She pulled out a sticky glob of dough. "This stuff keeps popping up all over the place. Every time I turn around I'm picking another piece out of something."

"I know what you mean," I said. I had dumped the dough from my bag in a compost pile in our backyard and had cleaned out my bag as best I could. But the stuff turned up everywhere—little lumps that stuck to my pencils, my books, my lunch bags, everything.

"I must have left my notebook in the cooking room," Ashley said. "Come with me to get it. I'll give it to you, and you can add to it or change it. That will take less time than starting over."

We found the custodian, who let us in, and we closed the door behind us.

"Don't even turn on the lights," Ashley said as she went over to our kitchen. "It'll just take me a minute." I waited by the door.

All of a sudden I heard Ed and Iggy coming down the hall. I recognized Iggy's voice and Ed's snorting laugh. The last thing I wanted was to be caught alone with Ashley.

I rushed over to her. "Ashley," I whispered hurriedly. "We've got to hide. Iggy and Ed are coming. I don't want them to find us alone in here."

"Why not?" she asked. "We're only here to get my notebook."

"I know that. But if they find us together—alone—that whole thing with Ed's graffiti and the teasing will start. I can't go through that again."

I could hear the custodian turning the key in the lock. "Please?"

She frowned. "Oh, I guess so. But where are we going to hide?"

"Come on," I said, practically dragging her. "There's the closet that all the mops and brooms are in. Hurry up."

Just as we squeezed into the closet, the custodian opened the door and turned on the lights. "I thought I just let two other kids in here," I heard him say. "They must have left. Just turn off the lights and close the door when you leave. Will you be long?"

"Nope," Ed said. "What we have to do won't take any time at all."

I had the broom closet door open a crack so we would get some air.

"What are they doing?" Ashley whispered. "We finished the breads today. There's no reason for them to be here."

"Maybe they forgot something," I whispered back. "Shhhh, they'll hear you."

"I hope they hurry up. It's stuffy in here."

Through the crack in the door I saw Iggy open his dirty yellow book bag. "What's first?" he asked.

"Give me the snakes," Ed said. "We'll do them in Jen and Sue's kitchen. They'll scream like mad."

Iggy took three long colored snakes out of his bag, the kind with springs that jump out of a can when you open it. Ed emptied the sugar out of their tin canister into a plastic bag and hid it in the cupboard while Iggy shoved the snakes into the canister. "That's one," Iggy said and grinned.

"Let's hide the plastic rat in Peter and Aggie's kitchen. She thinks she's such a terrific cook. That should upset her."

"Who gets the rubber band?" Ed asked. "Want to rig Ashley and Murphy's sink again? It worked like such a charm last time. Wasn't that a great fight they got into? Murphy got sprayed first, and then he turned around and hit Ashley."

They were practically falling on the floor from laughing. I was about to rush out of the closet and punch them both in the nose, but I could feel Ashley holding me back.

"Nah," Iggy said. "Let's do it in Steffie and Michael's kitchen. Maybe they'll think Ashley and Murphy did it. Then that'll start a double war between friends. I got some new rubber bands. They look practically invisible."

"So, what's left?" Ed asked. "What do you have for Murphy and Ashley?"

"Magic crystals," he said. "They look just like salt, but when they're in boiling water for a while, they turn bright green. It's vegetable dye, so it can't hurt anyone, but it looks terrible. I'll put it in their salt shaker, and they'll end up with a pot of bright green soup. That should get them fighting again.''

Ashley sucked in her breath, and I could feel the heat of her anger.

When they were done in our kitchen, Iggy zipped up his bag, looked around, and said, "There. Mrs. Barbage wants a grand finale, she'll get one. It's a week before we all have to cook again, and by that time no one will suspect that we had anything to do with this. I put a couple of fake plastic cockroaches under our sink, so we can holler and scream along with everybody else."

"I can't wait," Ed said as he shut off the light. "It'll be more exciting than fireworks on the Fourth of July."

When we heard the door close, Ashley and I stumbled out of the broom closet. We sat at the table in our kitchen, too amazed at what we had seen and heard to talk.

"I can't believe it," Ashley finally said. "I had always heard about Iggy and his practical jokes, but I never realized . . ." Her voice trailed off, and she sat there, just shaking her head.

I started to think about Iggy. "You know," I said quietly, remembering that stupid stink bomb I had planted, "if I hadn't been so worried about what Iggy thought of me, I probably never would have—"

Ashley interrupted me. "I'm sorry about blaming you for the sprayer," she said. "I should have known it wasn't you."

"And I'm sorry I squirted you," I said. "But I really thought you put the rubber band on our sink."

"And you know what else?" Ashley said. "If we hadn't been so mad at each other because of all the stuff Iggy did, I'll bet we could have made a perfect bread. On our own, I mean."

We both stopped talking for a while and sat there, thinking.

"What do you think we should do?" I asked Ashley. "Tell Mrs. Barbage?"

"Iggy and Ed will just deny it. They put the roaches under their sink so they'd look like victims, too." She suddenly opened her eyes extra wide, like some fantastic idea had zapped into her brain. Then she started to grin. "I know what we could do," she said.

Suddenly the same wonderful idea struck my brain. It was like two brilliant minds tuned to the same wavelength. "Let's go for it," I said as we walked toward Peter and Aggie's kitchen. "Iggy and Ed want fireworks? They'll get fireworks."

CHAPTER
SEVENTEEN

Ashley and I spent almost the entire weekend planning Adopt-a-Farm/Trash-a-Thon. We called everyone in our class we thought would be interested, set up a meeting for Monday after school, made up pledge sheets, and called Farmer Brown to tell him about our plans for next Sunday. He was so happy that he said he'd treat everyone who helped to deluxe ice-cream sundaes.

During our last phone call Sunday night, Ashley asked, "What about our soup? Have you given any thought to what we might make?"

"No," I said. "But it had better be something pretty terrific. Something that will impress Mrs. Barbage. If I don't get at least a B in cooking, it'll keep me off the honor roll."

"Me, too," she said. "Let's do some research next week."

"Maybe we could go to the Westford library one afternoon if we don't find anything at school," I suggested.

"What if Iggy and Ed see you with me?" she asked.

"Who cares?" I answered. "I'm tired of worrying about what other people think, especially people like Iggy and Ed. It's time to worry about me for a change—and what's important. Like grades. And not hurting other people for stupid reasons," I added.

On Monday Ashley and I gave our report. We told the class that sixteen more kids had signed up to help, and we showed them the pledge sheet we had designed.

"I'll have lots of them photocopied," Mrs. Barbage said. "You can pass them out at your meeting this afternoon. Dr. Harder is making an announcement on the P.A., so you might get more kids who are interested. And you can use my room—I'll come to your meeting, too."

Iggy and Ed were the only two who didn't seem interested. They were drawing pictures and passing notes. But we didn't need them anyway.

"Shouldn't we make some posters?" Steffie suggested. "We could hang them in school and at The Sundae School and maybe in some store windows around town to let people know what we're doing. If they know how hard we're working on this, maybe they'll help by not littering."

"That's a great idea," Ashley said.

"If we're going to make posters, let's think of a different name for our project," Peter said. "Adopt-a-Farm/Trash-a-Thon is too long."

"Let's see," I said. "We're collecting the trash at The Sundae School next Sunday. . . . How about calling it 'Super-Trash Sunday'?"

106

Everybody cheered. I bowed to all my fans, smiling modestly. Even Ashley applauded the new name.

The class spent the rest of the week in cooking class deciding what dish to cook. Ashley and I researched soup. We found all kinds: the usual ones like chicken noodle and vegetable and tomato; and some not-so-usual like carrot-curry and cold yogurt-cucumber and potato-cheddar cheese. We even found something called mulligatawny that had chicken and apples and all kinds of spices. But we found nothing that we thought was special enough or creative enough to get us the great grade we wanted.

Meanwhile, for three days after school, we held Super-Trash Sunday meetings. Twenty-eight of us made posters that said things like SAVE THE EARTH, IT'S THE ONLY ONE WE HAVE; EARTH DAY IS EVERY DAY; PICK UP YOUR TRASH—EVERY LITTER BIT HELPS, and ADOPT A WILD CHILD—CONTRIBUTE TO SUPER-TRASH SUNDAY. And every day after the meeting we all spent a little more time collecting pledges from our families, our friends, and our neighbors.

By Thursday in cooking class we knew Super-Trash Sunday was going to be a super-terrific success.

"You can't imagine how proud I am of you," Mrs. Barbage said. "Just look at all these posters. Are you planning another meeting for this afternoon?"

"No," Ashley said. "We told everyone that yesterday was our last. We're all prepared."

"Good," Mrs. Barbage said. "Let's plan to hang some of these posters around school tomorrow and the rest around Westford on Saturday morning. That way the whole town will be aware of what we're trying to do to save the farm. We'll leave them in my room for now. They'll be safe here. I would hate to have anything happen to them."

I heard Ed snort and mutter under his breath, "This whole thing is stupid. Don't you think so, Iggy?" Iggy just grunted.

"How are you all coming with your recipes?" Mrs. Barbage asked. "Don't forget, Monday is the Great Westford Elementary Cook-off. Write down any ingredients you need that we don't have in class and give them to me by Friday at the latest. Otherwise, I'll assume you have everything you need right here."

"We'd better decide on our soup," I said to Ashley. We must have looked through thirty different recipe books, and still nothing appealed to us. "We have to let Mrs. B. know what to buy."

"I know," Ashley said. "But I still can't decide. All those soups are so—ordinary."

"I wouldn't call cream-of-beet-greens ordinary."

"No," she said. "But it's just not original. I think we should make up our own recipe."

"Let's think of a soup that would impress Mrs. Barbage," I said.

"What? Recycled soup?" Ashley started to laugh at the idea.

Suddenly I had a brainstorm. "Why not?" I asked. "Why not make a soup that uses everybody else's leftover ingredients. We scrounge around all the kitchens and use anything edible that nobody else wants."

That got Ashley thinking. "Mrs. Barbage would love it," she said. "We would use only leftovers."

"Okay," I said. "Let's check her list to see what we're going to be graded on."

Ashley pulled the list out of her book bag, knocked off a little piece of dried dough, and spread it on the table. "Cost is first."

"If we use only recycled ingredients, our cost would be zero. What's next?"

"Nutritional value."

"Soup is always nutritional. And our soup will be four times more nutritional than anybody else's dish, because we'll be using something from everyone."

"So far it's A-plus soup," she said. "Taste is next. Do you think it'll taste good?"

"Sure," I said. "All those recipes we read for soup just dumped a bunch of stuff in water and cooked them to death. The more ingredients the better. What could go wrong? Add some spices and some salt and pepper and—it's soup. Besides, the taste grade is up to us."

"That's right," she said. "The last thing we'll be graded on is creativity of name. What do you think we should call it? Recycled Soup?"

"That's good," I said. Then my mind did a forward roll right into genius territory. "Better yet—how about . . . Mrs. Barbage's Garbage Soup!"

"Brilliant!" Ashley said. "We'll cook our way right into an A-plus. And it'll be so simple. Isn't it amazing what our minds can do when we work together?"

When we got back to our regular classroom after lunch, I found a note folded up on my desk. It looked almost like a sign, but it was hand-written in purple crayon in big block letters:

SECRET MEETING OF THE SUPER-TRASH SUNDAY
CLUB. MEET A HALF HOUR AFTER SCHOOL IN THE COOK-
ING ROOM. DON'T COME EARLY. DON'T BE LATE. FOL-
LOW DIRECTIONS.

DON'T COME EARLY was underlined five times. It
looked like something a second grader would write.

"Did you put this on my desk?" I asked Ashley.

"No, but I got one, too. What's going on? We didn't
call a meeting today. And what does it mean 'secret'?"

"I don't know, and what's all this about 'follow directions'? It sounds like something Mrs. Barbage would
say."

We hung around our classroom after school until it
was time to go to the meeting. When we got to the
cooking room, Mrs. Barbage was hurrying down the
hall, looking annoyed.

"Why didn't you two give me more notice?" she
asked. She was holding a sign like the one we had gotten. "You could have told me today in class instead of
sticking this under my windshield at lunch."

"We didn't call the meeting," Ashley said. "We got
the same note you did."

She seemed concerned. "Let's go in and see who else
shows up. Maybe there's a logical explanation." She
shoved the crayoned sign into the oversize bag she carried, pulled out a key, and opened the door.

The lights were out in the room, but in the shadows
we could see someone who had gotten there before us.
His back pocket was filled with Magic Markers, and he
was holding a red one open in his hand, standing over

110

one of our posters. Ed Witbread was adding graffiti to our hard work.

When he heard us come in, he wheeled around and faced us, his cheeks turning as red as the marker he held. "What are you doing here?" he asked.

"I might ask you the same question," Mrs. Barbage said, turning on the lights. "And what are you doing with those posters and those Magic Markers?"

When we saw one poster already marked up, the answer was obvious to all of us.

"I'm waiting for an explanation, Mr. Witbread," Mrs. Barbage said.

Ed's face burned brighter. "I . . . uh . . . I was just—"

I almost felt sorry for him. Maybe that's why I decided to bail him out. "You came to make some posters, didn't you, Ed?" I asked.

"What?" Ashley and Mrs. Barbage asked together.

"What?" Ed echoed.

"It's okay. I know you wanted to keep it a secret. But you don't have to be embarrassed. You just came here to make some more posters. You wanted to put those Magic Markers of yours to good use, didn't you?"

"I did?" he asked and gulped. "Yeah, you're right, I did."

"And you didn't want anyone to know. Especially Iggy. You didn't want him to tease you. But we won't tell a soul. Especially since the ten extra posters you make will probably be the best. Right?"

"Ten? You expect me to make ten posters by Saturday?"

"Okay," I said. "Make it five. Plus one for the one that you accidentally messed up. By tomorrow night.

Leave them on my porch. I'm sure Mrs. Barbage and Ashley will be willing to forget that we all saw you here." I turned to them. "Is that okay with both of you?"

Mrs. Barbage was trying hard to keep the expression on her face serious. I had a feeling she was biting the insides of her cheeks to keep from laughing. "I know the problems of peer pressure, Ed. Your secret is in good hands." She walked over to a cabinet, pulled out six pieces of poster board, and handed them to Ed. "Provided, of course, we like your posters. You do get my meaning, don't you?"

Ed looked like he wanted to throw a tantrum. But he had been caught red-handed, and he knew it. "You'll like them," he said, putting the cap on the red marker and sticking it in his back pocket. "But you won't tell, will you?"

Mrs. Barbage smiled. "Never. As long as you put your Magic Markers to good use only from now on."

As Ed left the room, I pulled the purple-crayoned sign out of my back pocket. "I wonder who we have to thank?" I asked.

"We'll probably never know," Mrs. Barbage said. "But somebody did us a big favor."

CHAPTER EIGHTEEN

I woke up at six-thirty Sunday morning. Usually I like to sleep until at least nine o'clock, but this was such a special day, I couldn't wait to get up and get going. Ed had delivered his six signs Friday night as promised, and they looked terrific. The Super-Trash Sunday club had spent Saturday morning hanging posters all over town. When the manager of a local supermarket read the poster we put in his window, he donated ten boxes of big black garbage bags for us to use.

Peter, Michael, Greg, and I walked together to The Sundae School. The first thing I wanted to do was find Wobbles. I had thought about checking on him a couple of times during the week, but I was afraid to. If he was sick, there wasn't much I would be able to do about it. I just kept hoping that our clean-up project wasn't too late for him.

When I got there, I didn't see him, and I didn't have time to look for him. More than fifty people including time to look for him. More than fifty people including some adults had come to help. Ashley and I organized everybody into teams, collected the pledge sheets from the kids in the club, and passed out trash bags to everyone. Mr. and Mrs. Barbage were there, too, dressed in their old clothes, to help us.

Before we started, Mr. Barbage had an announcement. "I have made arrangements for a truck to pick up all the bags you collect and deliver them to the dump," he told everyone. "Keep cans and bottles separate so we can recycle them."

We all put on gloves, grabbed our bags, and started to pick up garbage. I kept looking for Wobbles, but I couldn't see him with the other ducks, and I started to think maybe he didn't recover.

About an hour later the area I was working on had been picked clean. People were starting to spread out, working on some of the back areas of the farm. I took a clean bag and decided to go to the end of a large wooded area and work my way back. No one else had gone that way, so I figured I could fill a bag in no time.

When I came to a fence near the edge of The Sundae School property, I saw someone in the distance. As I got closer, I realized that it was Iggy Sands, carrying a garbage bag. He was probably planting stink bombs or setting up traps to go off when the kids started picking up back here.

I ducked behind a tree to watch.

It looked like he was taking something out of his garbage bag and spreading it around. I knew it! He was sabotaging our project. Here we were, breaking our

114

backs picking up litter and trash, and there he was, making more work for us.

Then I saw something that made me lose my cool completely. Next to him was Wobbles, eating out of Iggy's hand. It was one thing to make a mess. But to poison my duck? I was ready to kill him.

I left my garbage bag behind the tree and went charging up to him. When he saw me, he shoved his bag behind his back.

I stood in front of him, fuming, waiting for him to say something.

He grinned sheepishly. "Hi, Murphy," he finally said. "I didn't think anybody would be back here."

"I'll bet you didn't," I said. "Listen, Iggy, I've put up with a lot from you. But enough is enough. We worked too hard on this project to let someone like you or Ed ruin it. And what are you feeding my duck? He's been sick, you know."

He reached down and scratched Wobbles' neck. "You mean old Pork Belly here? He's not sick. Not anymore."

"So what are you feeding him?" I wasn't going to let Iggy wiggle his way out of this one.

"You mean this?" he asked as he slowly opened his hand. "It's a special mixture of food pellets and medicine. A man at the pet shop told me they might help a sick duck. It took me almost a week to get old Pork Belly here to eat them."

"Yeah, right! And what are you doing here? What's in that bag? Stink bombs?"

"What bag?" he asked, trying to hide it behind him.

"This one," I said, reaching around behind him and

wadded-up paper. Thinking he was hiding something underneath it, I dug to the bottom but came up with nothing but handfuls of cigarette butts, aluminum tops, and small pieces of plastic. There were even a couple of chewed-out pieces of gum.

Then I looked around us. For as far as I could see, the ground looked spotless—almost like a vacuum cleaner had been over the whole area. In the distance I could see a couple of bulging black garbage bags stacked under a tree.

I stared at Iggy, shocked, but he was looking at the ground, embarrassed. At least I thought he was, except that I had never seen Iggy Sands look embarrassed.

"You've been collecting garbage, too, haven't you?" I finally asked.

He was still looking at the ground. "I got here real early. I did the whole back section. I wanted to be gone before you all came. I didn't want anyone to know."

"Is Ed here, too?" I asked.

"Ed? Nah. He thinks the farm is for sissies." Then he looked at me and frowned. "And I agree with him, you know. It *is* for sissies. Listen, Murphy. I've got to go. Do me a favor, huh? Take the bags back. No one has to know about this."

"But I can't take credit for your work," I said.

"Sure you can. It would ruin my reputation if any of the guys found out. You can understand that, can't you?"

"I guess so," I said, thinking about how Iggy had almost ruined mine. But that was only because I gave in to him. I should have ignored his teasing. And I never

116

in to him. I should have ignored his teasing. And I never should have let him talk me into that stink bomb. Because I'm not Iggy. And Iggy's not me.

He reached into his back pocket and pulled out a dirty sheet of paper that was all folded up. Out of another pocket he pulled an envelope filled with crumpled dollar bills and a lot of change. "I put your name on the pledge sheet, Murphy. I was going to leave it in your desk tomorrow. There's not a lot of money there, but I made people pay in advance."

I opened my mouth to say thank you, but the look on his face told me he didn't want thanks. I looked around and saw Ashley headed our way. "You'd better go, Iggy. I'll take care of this." He just nodded his head and hurried away.

"Wasn't that Iggy?" Ashley asked as she came up to me.

When I didn't answer, she said, "Well, whatever he was up to, I hope you got rid of him."

I opened up the folded pledge sheet Iggy had given me and looked at it. At the top of the page, in big block letters in purple crayon, was written MURPHY DARINZO.

Ashley looked at the paper, at the envelope filled with money, and then at me. "Iggy?" she asked.

I nodded.

"That was nice of him."

"Do me a favor and don't say that, Ashley. I think the last thing Iggy wants is for us to think he's nice."

CHAPTER NINETEEN

Ashley and I went back to where everyone was bringing their garbage bags to be collected by the trucks. I got Peter to help me bring in the bags Iggy had collected. "How'd you do so many?" Peter asked.

"Just call me Super Trashman," I said.

We separated all the bottles and the cans from Iggy's bags so they could be recycled, tied up all the garbage bags, and spent the next hour feasting on the biggest sundaes we had ever seen. It was like a big party, but I kept wondering what would happen to the farm in the future. Would people just make a mess again? Would it end up being sold and turned into condominiums? I had happy and sad feelings, all mixed together.

Before we left, Mrs. Barbage called the cooking class together. "You've all done a wonderful job. But don't forget that tomorrow is the Great Westford Elementary Cook-off. I've made arrangements with your teacher to have you spend the whole morning in cooking class.

118

That way you won't be rushed, and we can enjoy our meal for lunch."

As we were leaving, Mrs. Barbage called Ashley and me aside. "You are the only two who didn't give me a list of ingredients to buy."

"We're all set," I said. "We don't need anything."

A look of concern crossed her face. "No meat? Or vegetables? You'll need more than hot water and spices. And I do want you to make a good soup."

"It's all under control," Ashley said. "We'll have everything we need."

"As long as you're sure," she said and left.

I was about to leave, too, when Ashley grabbed my arm. "Listen, Murphy," she said. "I've been thinking about this soup thing. Are you sure we'll have enough stuff to put in it? What if the other kids don't want to give up any of their ingredients?"

"Mrs. Barbage always buys extra," I said. "But if it'll make you feel better, check out whatever leftovers your mother has at home. I'll do the same. Bring in any extra food you can, and we'll dump it all in the soup. Believe me—Mrs. Barbage's Garbage Soup will be the best!"

When cooking class started on Monday, Ashley and I looked over the stuff we had brought in. I had a couple of wrinkled-looking potatoes that my mom wanted to throw out, some onions that had started to grow in the pantry, a hunk of cheese, and some celery greens. Ashley had some leftover baked beans, a hunk of meat loaf, and a can of stewed tomatoes ("I know they're not exactly leftovers," she explained, "but no one in our

119

house eats stewed tomatoes, so they would eventually get thrown out'').

When I asked her if she got the beans and meat loaf out of the garbage, she looked like she wanted to hit me. But then she laughed. I guess her sense of humor had returned along with our friendship.

"You put some water in a big pot and start chopping up the potatoes and the cheese," I said to her. "I'll see what I can round up from the other kitchens." I was about to leave on my mission when I turned back to her and said, "If that's okay with you."

"Get some good stuff, O brave hunter," she said and giggled.

I took a big bowl and stopped at Iggy and Ed's first. They gave me a hunk of ground-up turkey, some green pepper, and a whole bulb of garlic. I said thanks and was about to leave when Ed headed for the sink. I stopped to watch. He turned on the faucet, and the sprayer caught him right in the face.

"Hey, what the—" Ed spluttered as Iggy rushed toward him. I guess Ed thought Iggy had rigged it, so he grabbed the sprayer and shot Iggy.

Mrs. Barbage pushed past me. "Not again!" she hollered. "Now, that's enough. Let's just get back to business."

I left Iggy and Ed arguing while Mrs. Barbage was working to get them under control.

My next stop was Jen and Sue's kitchen. They were in charge of salad, and they had a whole counter full of stuff—apples, grapes, pears, carrots, raisins, and three kinds of lettuce. "We've got more than we need," Jen said. "Help yourself, Murphy."

As I stuck some of each thing in my bowl, Sue asked, "Want some walnuts? I'm cracking them now."

"No, thanks," I said. Somehow I didn't think nuts would do much for soup.

At Peter and Aggie's I added Chinese vegetables, two chicken wings, and a couple of chunks of beef to my collection. Aggie was busy chopping something, and Peter was busy watching.

"What's your job?" I asked.

"Chief taster," he said and burped. "Aggie's making three different kinds of appetizers. I'm supervising. When she needs something, I hand it to her." He smiled and wiped his brow. "It's a tough job."

"Hang in there," I said, patting him on the back. "I'm sure you'll survive."

Michael and Steffie, the dessert team, were rolling out some kind of dough. A frying pan and some oil stood on the counter waiting to be used. They were both wearing the heavy plastic goggles and the white lab coats we had to use when we deep-fried—safety precautions so that we wouldn't get spattered with hot grease.

They had nothing I could use for soup, but my bowl was already filled to the top. I had to walk slowly so that nothing would spill.

On my way back to our kitchen, I stopped once more at Iggy and Ed's. They were still bickering with each other but obviously hadn't yet figured out what had happened.

"Hey, Iggy," I said, putting my bowl on their counter. "Could I borrow a cup of sugar?"

He looked at me a little strangely but said, "Sure." I

watched with delight as he pulled out the sugar canister, opened the top, and hollered as three colored snakes sprang out at him. "Thanks, anyway," I said as I left. "I just remembered—we don't need any sugar for our soup."

It didn't take a genius to figure out what had happened, and I'm sure Ed and Iggy finally realized what was going on. As Ed opened the cabinet, he said to Iggy, "I smell a rat."

I started to chuckle as I went back to Ashley.

She had a big pot of water boiling on the stove, the potatoes and carrots cut up, the hunk of cheese shredded, the stewed tomatoes open. As I emptied the bowl of stuff on the counter, she looked worried. "I don't know, Murphy. Maybe this wasn't such a good idea. Are you sure it'll taste all right?"

I started dumping the strange assortment of ingredients into the pot—baked beans and raisins and apples and pears and chicken wings and beef and ground-up turkey and onions and tomatoes and lettuce and peppers and cheese. "The way I figure it, Ashley, is that Mrs. Barbage never tasted anything we cooked before. She certainly won't start now. And if anyone else in class tastes it, they wouldn't dare say it isn't good. How much of this garlic do you think I should put in?" I asked as I ripped the cloves apart.

"I don't know," she said. "All of it, I guess. What about these white grapes? Are they going in, too?"

"Of course," I said. "What would Mrs. Barbage's Garbage Soup be without a whole bunch of grapes?"

CHAPTER TWENTY

How's the soup look, Ashley?" I asked. She had taken the cover off the pot and was stirring it with a long wooden spoon.

"I don't know," she said. "It smells kind of funny, and the grapes keep popping up, floating on top."

I walked over and looked in the pot. What I saw resembled a clogged sink with pale white things bobbling on the top. "The grapes look like eyeballs," I said.

"I'm going to have trouble eating this," Ashley said. "I just hope I don't throw up."

"I'll bet it tastes better than it looks," I said.

"I hope it tastes better than it smells," she answered. "Oh, well, I guess I could eat anything if it meant getting a good grade."

"That's the spirit," I said.

Mrs. Barbage went from kitchen to kitchen, checking on our progress, and when she felt we were all ready, she stood in the center of the classroom and clapped her hands. "All right, everyone," she said. "Time for the big feast. Finish setting up, and we'll all meet in Peter and Agnes's kitchen—for appetizers."

Three covered dishes sat on Peter and Aggie's table. We all gathered around, and Peter said, "We have created three appetizers. The first is"—he paused as he pulled the cover off the first dish—"egg rolls. And the second is—sesame chicken wings. And finally—beef kabobs with peanut sauce." He looked like a proud father showing off triplets. Aggie stood in the background, smiling.

Anyone who wanted to taste was allowed to, and in no time flat, every egg roll, chicken wing, and beef kabob had disappeared. Aggie had really outdone herself. I was annoyed that Peter was getting so much credit, but he was my best friend, so I tried not to let it show. The only one who didn't eat anything was Mrs. Barbage. Ashley and I took that as a good sign.

"On to the salad course," Mrs. Barbage said, and we headed for Jen and Sue's.

"We call it Sassy Salad," Jen and Sue said together. Then Jen explained, "It's a combination of fruit salad and Waldorf salad, and we created our own dressing. It has hot pepper in it."

Again everyone tasted, but not quite as enthusiastically. The hot pepper left a tingling sensation in my mouth.

"Soup's next," Mrs. Barbage said. "Let's see what kind of a treat Ashley and Murphy have cooked up."

We ladled out a couple of bowls of soup, but no one made a move to pick up a spoon. It was the color and thickness of mud on a rainy day. Ashley and I tried to sound enthusiastic. "Who wants to try some?" I asked.

"I'm kind of full," Peter said.

"I'm saving my appetite for dessert," Michael said.

Mrs. Barbage looked at the bowls and then at us. "What, exactly, is it?" she asked.

"Mrs. Barbage's Garbage Soup," Ashley said. And we explained our recipe.

"What an interesting idea," she said. "But how does it taste? After all, when we are preparing something to eat, taste has to be one of our main considerations."

I took a big spoonful. What passed over my tongue and down my throat tasted a lot like what it looked like—mud. Except for the strong garlic taste and the lumps of raisins and grapes, I could have been eating a mouthful of mud.

Ashley choked down a spoonful and smiled. "It's very good," she said. "Do you want a taste?"

"I usually don't taste what my students cook. The calories, you know."

We sighed quietly in relief.

"However," she continued, "this time I will make an exception. After all, a soup that is named after me deserves a taste."

Ashley and I watched as Mrs. Barbage dipped a spoon in the gunk, put it in her mouth, chewed a while, and swallowed. She put the spoon down, closed her eyes, took a deep breath, and blew it out. Even from where I was standing, I could smell the garlic.

"I've never tasted anything quite like it," she said.

I was feeling pretty depressed as we headed for Iggy

and Ed's kitchen. We'd fail. The soup had a wonderful name and a terrible taste.

"And what have you two created?" Mrs. Barbage asked. I knew she wouldn't taste it. After our soup she'd probably never taste anything again.

Iggy grinned. "We have created Snake Guts for the main course," he said. Ed had piled bright green spaghetti onto a dish and was spooning over it a pale red sauce that had lumps of meat and peppers.

"How did you get the pasta to look so neon green?" Mrs. Barbage asked.

"We started out with spinach spaghetti," Ed said. "But when I added salt to the water, it turned a brighter green than we expected. Someone put food coloring in our salt," he added.

"But wouldn't you have noticed if the salt was green?" Mrs. Barbage asked, looking totally confused.

"It's a long story, Mrs. B.," Iggy said hurriedly. He picked up a fork and wound some spaghetti around it. "Who wants a bite?" he asked. "Snake Guts are dee-licious!" But everyone passed. Iggy and Ed were still slurping up their Snake Guts as we moved to the last kitchen for dessert.

Michael and Steffie had made Elephant Ears—fried dough covered with powdered sugar—and they really looked just like elephant ears. Everyone ate. Everyone except me. I had lost my appetite from an overdose of garbage soup.

We all went back to our kitchens to clean up. "If you have any food left," Mrs. Barbage said, "you can pack it up and take it home. Clean your kitchens and then gather around for your grades on this project."

126

Ashley and I didn't say a word as we cleaned up. We divided the rest of the soup into two containers to take home. I didn't ask Ashley what she was planning to do with hers, but I knew mine would end up where it belonged—in the garbage.

When we were all finished, we sat in a semicircle around Mrs. Barbage. "You've been a wonderful class," she said, "and I'm going to miss you. I believe you've all learned something. I tried not to interfere—even when I knew you were making big mistakes—because I believe children learn best by trial and error. Especially in cooking. Only when I saw a safety hazard did I feel it was necessary to step in."

She pulled out her grade book and opened it. "Since this has been a cooperative learning experience, I'd like to share your grades on the final project with the whole group."

I started to get nervous as she said, "Jen and Sue, you will make wonderful cooks. Maybe you could open a restaurant together because you both realize that cooperation is half the battle. Just go easy on the hot pepper in the future. Your grade is an A-minus."

"Michael and Steffie," she said. "You have both quietly cooked your way into an A. Good job."

Next she looked at Aggie and Peter and said, "Your appetizers were wonderful. And I would like to give you both an A." Peter grinned, sat back, and puffed out his chest. "But, Peter, I'm afraid that cooperation in cooking means more than setting the table, washing the dishes now and then, and eating." Shock showed on Peter's face. He opened his mouth to say something but changed his mind and shut it again.

"And Agnes," Mrs. Barbage said, "unless you plan to spend your life waiting on someone else, you should always insist on help from a partner. Therefore, I am giving both of you a B rather than an A on this project."

I couldn't believe it. Mrs. Barbage knew a lot more about what was going on in class than I had given her credit for.

I figured we were next, but she said, "Iggy and Ed. What can I say? You cooked a very interesting meal. Your Snake Guts were certainly creative, and from the way you two were eating, I'm sure they were tasty. However, the neon quality of the pasta was somewhat detracting, so I am giving you both a B-minus."

Ed and Iggy slapped each other a couple of high-fives. Those were probably some of the best grades those two would ever see in their whole school careers. And Ashley and I were headed for F's. Life just wasn't fair sometimes. Total humiliation was starting to creep over me.

Finally she turned to Ashley and me. The whole class was looking at us, and I was looking at the floor, my cheeks blazing.

"Murphy and Ashley," she began slowly. "I have never seen two students argue and fight as much as you did when we first started. You were like two strong ingredients simmering in the same pot, and I sometimes worried about what the outcome would be. But strong flavors in cooking don't always have to end in disaster. When they blend, they can be wonderful. Unfortunately, that didn't quite happen in your Mrs. Barbage's Garbage Soup. But unlike the soup, you two did learn to work together. And because the idea behind the soup was commendable, and because you have obviously

128

learned much more than cooking techniques, I have decided to give both of you an A-minus."

"Yessss!" I shouted, jumping up and punching a fist in the air. Ashley rushed over to me and gave me a big hug. In my excitement I hugged her back. Suddenly I realized everyone was looking at us, so I pushed Ashley away and said, "Quit it." But it was too late. Iggy and Ed were whispering and giggling and pointing at us.

When I got to school the next morning, a poster was pasted on the wall in front of our classroom. In big red letters someone had written YOU ARE ALL INVITED TO THE WEDDING OF MURPHY DARINZO AND ASHLEY DOUGLAS. BYOF—BRING YOUR OWN FOOD. On my desk was a blob of plastic barf with a note: "I ate some of your soup." As I was reading it, Drool stuck his dribbly face near me and made kissing sounds.

I'd have to wait until recess, but I knew I'd have to do something about it. I might end up bloody or dead, but I knew I'd have to fight.

In class it was back to business as usual. Our success in cooking, our success with Super-Trash Sunday seemed to sink into a sea of math and reading and spelling. In the middle of the morning Dr. Harder came on the P.A. and announced a special assembly for the whole school. As we walked toward the auditorium, I saw Ashley coming toward me, so I ducked behind a crowd of kids. I found a seat by myself way in the back and slumped down in it.

I don't think the teachers knew quite what was going on because things were a little disorganized. But finally everyone settled down, and Dr. Harder walked on stage in front of the closed curtains.

She thanked everyone for coming and then said, "I'd like to introduce some very important people who have asked us to gather here this morning—the mayor of the town of Westford, the governor of Connecticut, and the members of the city council."

As the curtain opened, she said the names of at least a dozen very important-looking people. I didn't pay too much attention because I figured it was going to be a boring assembly with long speeches. I slumped down even farther.

Then Dr. Harder said, "And now, I'd like to ask Town Councilman Robert Barbage to invite some very special students to join us on stage."

I hadn't noticed Mr. Barbage up there, and before I knew what was going on, I heard my name and Ashley's name being called along with all the kids from our cooking class. Even Ed and Iggy's names were called.

We all lined up on stage. Ashley managed to stand next to me with Iggy on my other side. There I was, caught between my two best enemies, in front of the whole school.

The governor took the microphone. "We are proud this morning to present these young men and women with special awards. It is because of their efforts that a little piece of our world has been saved." And he went on to explain how we organized Super-Trash Sunday and how we cleaned the farm and helped to save the animals. He even held up one of our posters—one that Ed had made—for the whole audience to see.

Then the mayor took the microphone and turned

toward us. "And because of your efforts, the town of Westford has decided to purchase The Sundae School as a park and a sanctuary. The owner is happy to sell it to us, and he has agreed to stay on to manage the farm and the ice-cream shop. Now—will Murphy Darinzo and Ashley Douglas please step forward."

Ashley and I looked at each other and walked toward the mayor. He shook our hands and said, "As organizers of the project, please accept these awards for outstanding service to the community and to the environment." He handed each of us a trophy that had a fat duck sitting on top of it.

The whole school stood up and applauded.

As we walked back to class, everyone crowded around us, wanting to see our awards and trophies. Even Ed and Iggy seemed to enjoy all the attention they were getting.

We came to one of Ed's wedding posters, and everyone stopped. Suddenly it got quiet. Ashley was standing next to me, and it looked like Drool was ready to start making his slurping noises.

All at once Ed reached up, pulled the sign off the wall, and ripped it in half. He turned to me and smiled. "You know what, Murphy?" he asked. "One thing I always admired about you—you got a great sense of humor."

I just grinned.

"Yeah," Iggy echoed. "I'm glad we have you for a friend."

About the Author

M. M. RAGZ is the writing coordinator for Stamford High School in Stamford, Connecticut. She literally does her writing on the run, developing story ideas while jogging. While her job with the school system keeps her busy teaching writing, conducting writing workshops and seminars, and giving book talks, Mrs. Ragz occupies her free time with a range of activities that includes watercolor painting, crafts, gardening, and summers on Cape Cod in Eastham. She holds three college degrees from the University of Connecticut and Fairfield University. She has traveled to Germany, Mexico, Greece, Britain, and the Caribbean.

She lives in Trumbull, Connecticut, with her husband, Phil, and their youngest son, Michael, who is the inspiration for many of Murphy's adventures. All of her books about Murphy, *Eyeballs for Breakfast*, *Eyeballs for Lunch*, *Sewer Soup*, and *Stiff Competition*, are available from Minstrel Books.

JAMIE GILSON KEEPS YOU LAUGHING!

____ **HOBIE HANSON, YOU'RE WEIRD** 73752-X/$2.95
Who said being weird isn't any fun? Hobie Hanson doesn't think so.

____ **DO BANANAS CHEW GUM?** 70926-7/$2.99
It's not a riddle, it's a test. And since Sam can't read, it's not as easy
as it looks!

____ **THIRTEEN WAYS TO SINK A SUB** 72958-6/$2.99
Substitute teachers are fair game—and the boys and girls of Room 4B
can't wait to play!

____ **4B GOES WILD** 68063-3/$2.95
The hilarious sequel to THIRTEEN WAYS TO SINK A SUB—Room 4B
goes into the woods at Camp Trotter and has a wild time!

____ **HARVEY THE BEER CAN KING** 67423-4/$2.50
Harvey calls himself the Beer Can King, and why not? He's the proud
owner of 800 choice cans. A collection his dad would love to throw in
the trash!

____ **HELLO, MY NAME IS SCRAMBLED EGGS** 74104-7/$2.99
Making new friends should always be this much fun.

____ **CAN'T CATCH ME, I'M THE GINGERBREAD MAN**
69160-0/$2.75 Mitch was a hotshot hockey player, a health food nut
and a heavy favorite to win the National bake-a-thon!

____ **DOUBLE DOG DARE** 67898-1/$2.75
Hobie has got to take a risk to prove he is special, too!

____ **HOBIE HANSON, GREATEST HERO OF THE MALL** 70646-2/$2.95
Hobie is determined to be a hero—even if he's over his head in
trouble!

____ **DIAL LEROI RUPERT, DJ** 70252-1/$2.75

____ **HOBIE HANSON IN STICKS AND STONES
AND SKELETON BONES** 74939-0/$2.99